HALFWAY TO HELL

By the same author

Day of the Lawless Gun

HALFWAY TO HELL

BLAKE MORGAN

A Black Horse Western

ROBERT HALE · LONDON

© Blake Morgan 1995
First published in Great Britain 1995

ISBN 0 7090 5479 3

Robert Hale Limited
Clerkenwell House
Clerkenwell Green
London EC1R 0HT

The right of Blake Morgan to be identified as
author of this work has been asserted by him
in accordance with the Copyright, Designs and
Patents Act 1988.

Photoset in North Wales by
Derek Doyle & Associates, Mold, Clwyd.
Printed and bound in Great Britain by
WBC Ltd, Bridgend, Mid-Glamorgan.

ONE

It was approaching noon, and out of the cloudless blue of the sky the fiery sun burned down relentlessly on the parched valley plain. The speckle-bearded man and his mule might have been the only living creatures in this thirsty world. The old buffalo wallow two miles back had been dried to an iron hardness, and Rufus Jepp doubted that he'd find any water between here and the town of Victory, which was hidden beyond the horizon, and he just had one full canteen left. At least he'd found the shade he was looking for, though; a big upjutting rock like a single tooth, leaning forward just enough to cast a shadow where he and the animal could get some respite from the fire in the sky.

As they came into that skimpy snatch of shade, he forced his aching muscles into movement, and eased himself off the animal's back. He dragged a few greentops and root vegetables out of a sack slung amongst the other baggage, and dropped them on the ground. There was moisture enough in them to keep the mule alive. The rock was too hot to lean against, so he squatted down, and took a few careful sips from the canteen.

It had been the driest, hottest season anyone in

Brady County had known for a long time. Day after day the handful of small settlements and towns sweltered under an unclouded sky, and nobody could move an inch without raising a cloud of thick, choking dust. Wells which had seemed inexhaustible began to dry up, and small boys looked wistfully at their fishing poles, and wished that maybe tomorrow some miracle would bring rain and the creeks would start to fill again.

Rufus Jepp came from Bethel, so he knew all about praying for miracles. It was a tumbledown kind of place, a shanty town in the middle of nowhere where every man carried a Bible in his pocket and was pledged to carry the Lord's Word out to the ungodly in a land where there were twenty saloons to every church. Sure, he knew that a sinful old cowhand who'd got religion was a kind of joke, and a travelling preacher like him rarely had a congregation you could count on your right hand. Since he'd lost a finger on that hand when he'd roped a frisky steer and it had run away with him that wasn't saying too much. But that's what he did now for a goodly part of the year, and he knew the Good Lord wasn't laughing at him.

Travelling this country was as grained into his nature as the dirt under his fingernails. Rufus Jepp knew this land well, had known it since he'd been fourteen years old. His pa had brought him out here in the days when there'd been a growing silver fever. Old Indian legends said that there was a silver seam up there wide as a river, and for a while rocky outcrops like the Hogtail Ridge had swarmed black with hopeful miners. Some had been lucky, most not, and his pa sure hadn't.

Broke his neck in a drunken fall leaving the boy to fend for himself.

Not good mining land, then, though it had sure as Sunday been buffalo country in those times; then the shabby herds had been hunted out of existence, and the cattlemen moved in. Most years there was enough rain to fill the water holes and to keep the grass growing; and a wide enough swathe of open range to satisfy the needs of the cattle. Then the cowmen had been followed by the homesteaders, hungry for their own slice of land.

Farmers and ranchers always made poor neighbours. To begin with, it was a time of fence-building and fence-cutting, fraying tempers, and angry words. Then a couple of years of low rainfall and drying winds had made things worse, with griping resentment changing to hatred.

Rufus Jepp recollected that time well. He'd been a cowhand back then, and like all punchers he was on the side of the ranchers who put money in their pockets. He'd done his share of stampeding steers into cropping fields, of filling up irrigation trenches which were draining the sluggish creeks. He'd ridden with a dozen men late at night past homesteads, firing his gun and bellowing threats like the rest of the night-riders. That's how it had been then. A man took sides, and acted the way he had to.

Some of the nesters quit quickly enough, bundling their few possessions onto bent-axled wagons, or rickety flat-bed carts and headed away from Brady County. Others stayed, and vowed they'd never be moved by the arrogant cattlemen. When men band together in a cause, they look for a leader, and the nesters found Professor

Polanski. Maybe he was a real Professor, Jepp never did know that for sure. It was said he'd been a teacher back in his own country, right on the eastern edges of Europe. There'd been some kind of revolution, and Polanski's side had lost, and he'd brought his family to the New World to start again.

When other men ploughed up their new land they'd set aside any large field stones to use later. On the flat where he'd settled, nestling up against the twisted rise of the Hogtail, Polanski found more than stones. Bones, that's what he started turning up, 'specially when he started digging deeper. Big bones they were, so old they'd turned to stone themselves. The little immigrant with the shock of white hair got real excited about those bones. The way he told it they belonged to animals which had grazed and hunted these plains thousands of years back.

Rufus Jepp had laughed like the rest of them, knowing the world just couldn't be as old as Prof Polanski said. Noah had never taken any giant lizards into the ark with him, that was for sure. They sure were big bones, though, and the biggest was the jawbone. Took two men to lift it and put it on a wagon to take it into the nearby town of Victory. A local businessman called Jude Wallis paid a few dollars for it, and had it displayed outside the hotel he owned. Ever after, that hotel was called the Jawbone, and the place where Polanski had his homestead was christened Jawbone Flat.

Thinking about all this now, Rufus Jepp's throat seemed to get even drier, and he risked another sip from his canteen. Prof Polanski might be interested in the past, but he also had a powerful interest in the present. He started stirring up the nesters with stories of what had happened back in his homeland, how the rich men and the bankers and the landlords and the shopkeepers had made life miserable for the poor people. Telling how it was much the same here now, and how oppressed folk should face up to those kind of men. He'd become the leader of the farmers, and a blacksmith name of Abel Cray had become his lieutenant, and between them they put a new spirit into the nesters.

It seemed like war was coming in that skin-blistering summer sixteen years ago, with the homesteaders standing their ground, vowing to protect their land against anything the ranchers could throw at them. Then one night it was all over. Polanski's cabin on Jawbone Flat caught fire and everyone inside the cabin, including Abel Cray the blacksmith, were fried to a crisp.

Rufus Jepp screwed the cap tight on his canteen, and pushed himself to his feet. The nester army had lost its leaders, and the threatening war never came. Soon after that the rains arrived and tempers cooled down, and though differences were never exactly sorted out, burning enmity mellowed into a grudging acceptance on both sides.

The living was never easy on this marginal land, but it was never as tough as it might be. The nesters kept advancing in a slow, steady flood, and every year the open range shrank a touch more. Now the living wasn't easy. A couple of dry years had been followed by this one. Now all the earth's moisture was being sucked out by the sun, and the land was starting to break up, and the shallow grass-roots had nothing to hold them. Too much of the land had been scarred by the plough, turning to dust in the incessant heat, and out on the range the herds had to trek ever further for any sort of feeding, or watering.

Further north the word seemed to have spread among the wolf population that there were easy pickings in open country. Growing numbers of them were appearing on the edges of the listless herds, and culling the weakest of the gloomy, ribby cattle. Maybe it wasn't all the fault of the farmers, but it was a damn sight easier to blame them than to blame anyone else.

Jepp remembered one thing he'd heard Prof Polanski say about how history always repeated itself. About how men always forgot what they'd learned. Back in Bethel they'd been talking about that, and Rufus Jepp had told the rest of the brethren something he'd never told anyone else. It was something he'd tried to forget by becoming a preacher and trying to show other folk the error of their wicked ways. Now, with war-clouds looming again, it was time he told the truth. Because maybe that way he could make sure that history didn't repeat itself.

He patted the neck of his weary, thirsty mule. 'Come on boy, we got God's work to do.'

TWO

Sweat rolled off his heavy jowled face as Deal Tyler strode into George's Bar in the town of Victory. His shirt clung like a rag to his broad back, and he plainly needed something cold to sluice some of the dust out of his throat. The late evening customers at the bar shifted instinctively to one side or the other as he came up. Beef profits were going to be skimpy this year, and ranchers like Tyler, for one, weren't any too happy about it. He was heading for sixty, but he still packed a powerful punch, and on a good day his temper was uncertain. At the end of what had plainly been a bad day, a rattlesnake would be safer company.

Gil Coker, the barman, was already setting out a glass of beer for him. The big rancher downed it in one, and made a sour face as if it was some foul-tasting medicine. 'Back east you can buy a beer that'd freeze your teeth outa your head,' he complained.

Somebody laughed, and Tyler fired him a gun-shot sharp glare. 'I wasn't making a joke, mister. Wasn't talking to you, neither.'

'Sure am sorry, Mr Tyler.' Because he was a farmer, and knew how men like Tyler were feeling, the man decided to get home and listen to his missus worrying about how they were going to feed the family if rain didn't come soon to save their crops.

After the second beer Tyler became calmer, if no less morose. 'One hell of a day. Lost two dogies to some old wolf we got roaming down near Hogtail Ridge.'

'Sure it was a wolf?' queried the barkeep. 'There's hungry folk out there, too.'

'Don't I know it,' muttered the rancher. 'Sure, it ain't only wolves after my beeves. But I seen the tracks, and I found what was left of the carcases. Sure as damnation was a wolf took 'em.' He shrugged. 'We'll get the varmint!'

The barkeep nodded encouragingly. 'Sure you will, Mr Tyler.'

The rancher's eyes narrowed. 'I don't recall asking for your opinion, Coker! Nor any kind of talk from you. Can't a man drink in peace no more?'

Coker mumbled some kind of apology, and shifted away. Now Tyler was left stranded; edgy and brooding, with only the glass in front of him for company. He'd been here before, sure enough. He'd seen thirsty seasons before; he'd lived through winters where half his herd had frozen to death where they stood. The world ran in cycles like that. Dorothy always reckoned that you couldn't know what was good if you'd never seen what was bad. She'd died long, long ago, though, and her picture might smile at him, but it couldn't talk to him and tell him how things would get better. How rain would come again, and his cattle would be barrel-fat, chewing up the lush buffalo grass the whole of each long, lazy day.

'Gimme another beer, Coker!' Tyler stared at the calendar nailed next to the big mirror and shook his head, 'Make it a whisky. And leave the bottle in front of me.'

There was more than one man in George's Bar who looked at the calendar too, and recollected what today's date would mean to the big rancher. Those men knew that old sorrow and new whisky made an explosive mixture in someone like Tyler. They sensed that before the night was out someone might be staggering homeward with a flattened nose, or a busted jaw. They'd sooner it wasn't them, and as the word rippled round George's Bar, Gil Coker watched his customers draining out into the night.

Jude Wallis sat on the verandah of his fine big house at the other side of town, staring at the moon, fanning himself with a newspaper. In the normal way he'd be praying for a breath of wind to help cool things down, but that'd only raise a cloud of suffocating dust and make things worse. By day, he was a swaggering, expensively dressed man of business. Not young anymore, maybe, but given a preserving coat of varnish by his money and his power. He owned, or part-owned most of the town that was worth owning. There was no shine to him right now. Stripped to his sweat-soaked undershirt and long-johns he felt like what he was, a man going to seed.

He glowered at the idea. He'd come a long way since he and his brother had set up a trading post alongside the way station that had been here before anything else. Couple of years after that they'd opened up a saloon, with ten girls working for them to provide lonely cowhands with the kind of comfort that couldn't come from a glass.

It was on the way to becoming a town, but still hadn't gotten itself a fixed name, though the Wallis brothers were starting to figure it should be called after them. They never could quite agree on whether it should be called Wallisville or Wallisborough, though. In the end the vexatious matter of the town's name was settled by the Sioux. In those days the tribes were getting agitated by the flood of cattlemen and settlers surging over their hunting grounds. Once the railroad started poking westwards they decided they'd had enough. One sunny spring day a sizeable bunch of them decided to ride into the nameless township and generally make it unfit for folk to live in.

The couple who ran the way station, and their three children died in the first few minutes of that sweeping, howling onslaught. A couple of braves hauled out the oldster manning the telegraph office and clubbed him to death. George Wallis, Jude's brother was busy serving a couple of homesteaders in the trading post. They all lost their lives and their hair.

The war party ran into a solid brick wall when they took on the saloon where Jude was having his work cut out coping with Deal Tyler and a crowd of his boys. His customers didn't take too kindly to having their entertainments interrupted by visitors wearing warpaint. For a few bloody hours the saloon became a fortress under siege. A dozen of the defenders, including two of the saloon girls, were dead at the end of it. Everyone else lived to tell the tale, managing to hold out until a detachment of cavalry arrived on the scene.

After that baptism of blood there was only one name to give the town. Victory, they called it, and on every anniversary of the battle they hauled the Stars and Stripes high, and celebrated their salvation.

Wallis stood up, suddenly restless, scratching himself. This blasted drought was beginning to nag at him. Takings were down in his stores, and in the saloon, and there'd been nobody staying in his hotel for six weeks or more. Folk were tightening their belts against hardships to come. He was kind of stretched himself in the money stakes; a few too many poker games going wrong, a couple of business deals in another part of the state had turned sourer than week-old milk. Willy Candell at the bank wasn't near so forthcoming as he'd been once upon a time, neither.

He stomped inside the house. There were two cures for that kind of morbidness, but he only had one of them close to hand. He grabbed the bottle of bourbon and poured himself a generous slug, slumping into a chair like a bag of wet sand.

'Well, there's a pretty sight!'

Wallis glared towards the doorway. He couldn't see so well without his eyeglasses, but he knew the sound of his own son's voice well enough. 'I thought you was planning on spending the evening at the Scales place. Go hold young Emmeline's hand and try a touch of sweet-talk, that's what you said.'

Wade Wallis ambled closer, and fetched himself a glass. 'Holding hands wasn't quite what I had in mind!'

'Leave some of that bourbon for me!' growled his father. 'And you talk respectful about Emmy. And mind how you treat her. Me and her pa go back a long way.'

'So you're always telling me,' retorted his son.

'Benton Scales saved my life that day.' Wallis sniffed. 'I'd have been fixed by that Sioux throwing-knife for sure if he hadn't dragged me away from that window.'

The Indian had shimmied right up to the saloon during a lull in the fighting. Wallis's back was to the window, and Scales, one of Tyler's crew then, had spotted the dark shape rising up outside. He'd yanked Wallis off his feet and the knife had sliced air instead of human flesh.

Wade lounged in a chair. He'd heard the story too often. 'I'm not so sure Emmy Scales is my kind of gal.'

'What in hell you got against her?' demanded Wallis incredulously. He'd been jawing with the manager of his general store a couple of weeks back when she'd sashayed in. Emmy had those same dark smouldering eyes which her ma had used to snare Benton; the same midnight black hair. The willowy grace in the way she carried herself, her smooth, leggy walk put him in mind of a young pine curving and swaying in a mountain wind. He gulped back his liquor at the very thought of her, and wished it was him and not his lazy-brained son courting the girl.

Wade was watching his father with a crooked, knowing smile. 'I do believe that gal's sending the sap rising through your branches, pa. Maybe you should take yourself over to the hotel quick. Pay a call on Trudi while the mood's in you.'

Wallis scowled. 'All that town gossip about me and Trudi is just that. Gossip. Works for me, that's all. And she's young enough to be my daughter.'

'And old enough to be your....'

The older man cut in quick. 'You just watch that tongue of yours, boy. And I said, what you got against Emmy?'

'That one's got some queer ideas about a whole lot of things, pa.' Wade shrugged. 'Guess all that fancy education she got back in Ohio has kind of turned her head.'

'Maybe, but she's still a woman!' grunted Wallis. 'And what's in her head don't come into it. It's time you settled. I figure on having me some grandchildren before they nail the lid down on me.'

Wade sniffed. 'I figure Emmeline Scales is more interested in writing her blasted book than helping you become a grandpappy.'

'What's that you say?' Wallis downed the last of his whisky, and thrust his glass out in the general direction of his son. 'Woman writing a book? What kind of book?'

'History book, she says.' Wade filled his father's glass. 'The true story of Victory or some such nonsensical idea.'

Wallis slumped back. 'Women ain't what they used to be. I always figured Benton Scales was kinda crazy sending her off to that ladies' college. History? That's something you know in here....' He tapped his head, 'Not something you read in books.'

'Well, I'll keep working on her. But it's kinda like trying to romance an old log of wood.' Wade lit himself a cigar. 'Was asking me what I knew about that ... Polanski business ... all those years ago. She's planning on riding over to his place on Jawbone Flat sometime.'

'Why'd she do that?' Wallis goggled. 'There ain't nothing there now. Nothing to see. All of that was over and done almost 'fore you and her was born.' He blinked uneasily. As far as he was concerned, there were some things in Victory's past that were best left buried. One of those was definitely the night that Prof Polanski's cabin got burned down.

'Young Emmy had best take care who she talks to 'bout that night, Wade,' he grumbled, after a long pause. 'There's some don't want to be reminded. Deal Tyler for one. There was five bodies dragged out of that place. One of them was his girl Charlotte.'

His son was listening intently. 'I know that. Though I still don't rightly know what it was all about.'

'And you don't need to know. Neither does Emmy!'

'Sixteen years today, Emmy told me. Since it happened. There was a drought that year, too, she says.'

'Guess there was.' Wallis swallowed hard. 'What happened then is best forgot. And how come Emmy's taking such an interest?'

'I told you, she's fixing on writing a book,' said Wade idly. 'Says her pa won't tell her much. That's how come she was asking me. Sure, I got hazy recollections about that night. But hell, I was only a sprig. All I know is that a cabin was burned down, and some folk got killed.' He studied his glass thoughtfully. 'I recall that ma got real upset.'

'Sure she did,' muttered Wallis. ''Specially on account of Charlotte.'

'So what was it all about, pa? I mean, Emmy's right on one thing. Nobody seems too keen on talking about it.'

'And that 'cludes me! I ain't talking about it, neither.' Wallis hurled the rest of his bourbon down his throat.

'There was some feller called Cray mixed up in it, too,' Wade went on thoughtfully, 'I got this picture of a real big feller in my head.'

'Big, sure. Town blacksmith. 'Mongst a whole lot of other things.' His son's questions itched at him like a hair shirt, and Wallis stood up. 'I'm surprised that Benton Scales ain't put a stop to Emmy fishing round in those waters. Won't do no good. Can't do no good. Polanski's dead. Charlotte Tyler's dead. And Cray, too!'

Sweat rolled off him. He had two memories which sometimes haunted him in nightmares. One of them was seeing what those savages had done to his brother George. The other was hearing that terrible howl of rage and grief which came from Deal Tyler's throat when the blanket was pulled away from the charred and blackened remains of his only child. He got a sudden soul-shivering notion that he was going to be visited by that kind of nightmare tonight. He figured he'd just as soon stay awake than have that happen.

Willy Candell slammed the last ledger shut and wiped the sweat out of his eyes. It was too late now. Tomorrow, he'd be out of a job. Once those fellers from the head office of the State Loan and Savings had got their spiky fingers into the pages of these ledgers, they'd soon be asking him none too politely about certain discrepancies.

He rocked back morosely in his chair. There'd been a time when this bank had been his, and his alone. William Candell, President of Victory's first bank; a man to respect. Cowmen brushed the dust from themselves before coming to see him; farmers scraped their boots clean before they trudged up his steps. Twelve months back the merger with the state banking corporation had seemed like a dandy idea; except it turned out that it was less of a merger, and more of a take-over, with him becoming no more than an employee. They'd let him be for the most part, and he'd been fooled into thinking that he could still shift money from here to there, make use of it for himself while it was doing nothing else in particular.

Now the moment of reckoning was heading for him with the speed of a wagon-team out of control. He'd made too many loans to himself; and he wasn't in any position to pay them back. His powerful days were gone. Those early days when the nesters found they needed more than hope and hard work to build up their mean little homesteads. Willy Candell made it sound so easy; made himself sound so generous. He handed over a roll of dollars, and they could buy seed and feed, and tools which didn't break in the unforgiving earth. All they had to do was sign their name on a piece of paper, or make a spidery cross if they couldn't do that much. Easy enough to pay it back when the living was smooth.

Not so easy when the sky stayed cloudless and times became tough. Those were the days when he'd have grown men sobbing in front of him, begging him not to foreclose on their loans. He didn't figure that sobbing and begging on his knees in front of the men from the Loan and Savings Corporation would do him a whole lot of good.

Loosing the collar of his shirt, he sopped up the sweat on his neck with a damp kerchief. Then he grinned suddenly. Bad times coming for him maybe, but there had been good times. Like when that respectable married lady had bought her man just a little more time. Maybe hunger had taken some of the meat off her, but she'd still been a fine-figured woman to share a man's bed, and do whatever he wanted. That was a night worth recalling. Hadn't done her husband a whole of good, though. Couple of weeks later he'd blasted his face away with a shotgun, and the woman had taken her kids back east.

Now, with the world drying-up and blowing dust, there'd be lines of men outside the bank every morning. Same story as it had been then: 'I just can't make this month's payment, Mr Candell. Just give me a little more time....'

No sun-weathered women in their Sunday finery had turned up yet, with their own special propositions, but he guessed they might have done. Well, he wouldn't be here to hear them after tomorrow. Such a blasted waste.

Candell's fingers drummed on the nearest ledger, and his eyes moved to the fancy calendar on his wall. He'd better savour this last day. Then, just like other men were doing across town, he realised that this date had another meaning, and despite the searing heat, the banker shivered, recalling how Abel Cray had stormed into this very office one day; thundering his contempt and his rage for how Candell had treated some now long-forgotten family of 'steaders. Willy Candell was a small, scrawny man; quaking behind his desk as the eyes of that big, angry blacksmith blazed at him.

It wasn't a memory Candell cared to dredge back. Anyhow, Cray was long gone. Nothing to fear from him now. The only thing to fear now was those tight-lipped, gimlet-eyed fellers from the Loan and Savings.

There was an uneasiness gnawing beaver-like inside him, though; the memory wouldn't go away. It clung to him, hanging on with sharp, painful claws. Cray's words echoing round his head: 'You'll burn for this, Candell. In hell. You hear. You'll be punished. Punished for all the wicked, cruel things you've done to decent folk.'

'You were the one that burned, Cray....' mumbled Willy Candell. 'Burned and black like a loaf left too long baking. Along with all the others in Polanski's Cabin.'

He shivered again. Well, maybe it was like that. There was a grave in the town cemetery all right. But there were those who opined darkly that the crumbling remains they'd put in that grave were just too damn skimpy to be all that was left of a big man like Abel Cray. That maybe he wasn't dead. That maybe one day he'd come back.

Just a lot of fool-headed talk, of course.

From the room next door Emmy Scales heard the heavy snores of her father. Nothing seemed to stop him sleeping. She sat there a while flicking through the pages of a book; the moon was so bright tonight there was scarcely any need of the lamp burning by her bedside. After a few minutes, though, she swung her legs off the bed, and fetched a loose shirt, and a riding skirt out of the closet.

Mrs Bax the housekeeper was still in the kitchen. 'Now where d'you think you're going off to, missie?'

'Thought I'd take a ride. The gelding hasn't been out for a couple of days.'

The elderly woman sniffed disapprovingly, 'You've not told your father 'bout this, have you?'

'No, Mrs Bax, I haven't,' Emmeline admitted. 'And I'm surely not going to wake him up to tell him. I'm only going out as far as Jawbone Flat.'

The housekeeper blinked. 'Well, I guess you can't come to no harm. It's bright as day out there. Just don't stay out too long, else I will have to wake Mr Scales.'

As she'd suspected there were still plenty of her father's hands drifting round outside, only too willing to saddle her horse up for her, to offer to keep her company, make sure the wolves didn't get her. By the time she rode out of the ranch-yard there was quite a crowd of them gathered round. There was nothing to fear from them. If any of them laid so much as a finger on her, they knew that Benton Scales would half-kill them. She was flattered by their attention and their admiration, even if sometimes it did get wearisome being a walking sideshow for every lonely cowhand in Brady County.

She'd imagined it might be cooler out here in the open, away from the ranch but the heat was still rolling off the parched earth. Still, the gelding trotted along cheerfully enough, following the course of the dried up creek. She remembered plenty of times when she'd seen that creek just about bursting its banks as it danced noisily down to the river.

A giggle burst out as she recalled again that day she'd been out on her old pony and come upon a gang of local boys swimming here, every one as naked as the day their mothers bore them. Quite some eye-opening for a fourteen year old girl!

Her smiled curdled a little. Wade Wallis had mentioned that very same event when he was round earlier. According to him they'd all stood there on the creek bank, daring her to look at them, daring her to come swimming with them. The way she pictured it, she'd sat defiantly astride her pony, right on the edge of the bank, and they'd all stayed shivering in the water, faces redder than a winter-setting sun, begging her to ride off.

'It ain't decent, you sitting there staring at us, Emmy Scales!' one of them had yelled. That boy had been Wade Wallis, she was sure.

She hadn't told him that, not tonight. He'd only deny it, and that would make one of them a liar, and where was the point in riling Wade? She didn't like him, he was too much like his father, with his sly, knowing eyes. She'd carried on being real pleasant to him, though, telling him about her plans to write herself a book about the history of the township of Victory.

'My principal at the college put the idea into my head.'

'She'd be a lady?' Wade had queried with interest.

'Of course! We only had women teachers. Only

man working in the college was our caretaker. Sixty if he was a day!'

'Don't sound natural to me,' he'd observed, edging a little closer along the sofa.

Determined to finish what she was saying, she'd stood up and gone to sit in a chair. 'She said that the West was changing fast and that maybe someone should start writing things down about it before they all got forgotten.'

'What kind of things? Battle of the Little Big Horn? Kit Carson? Davy Crockett? Heck, Emmy, nobody's ever gonna forget all those. They don't need writing down.'

Emmy had given a shake of her head. 'Not the big things, Wade. Not the big Indian battles, or the frontier heroes. But the ordinary things. Small towns. Small people. Like us here in Victory.'

He hadn't laughed, for sure, but he'd plainly thought it was a crazy notion, especially for a woman. She rubbed the gelding's neck. 'Thing was, he didn't say what he meant,' she murmured. 'And I won't trust a man who doesn't do that.' The horse's ears clicked back as if was listening, and she turned him away from the course of the creek, towards the dark tangle of scrub-oak, elder and birch which was Jawbone Flat.

She found the ruins of the cabin without too much trouble, even though it was a good few years since she'd been here. Leaving the gelding to wander, she picked her way amongst what was left of the rotting, scorch-marked walls. Five people had died here, trapped in a flimsy cabin nailed together from rough planking, including Deal Tyler's daughter and the town blacksmith.

There were all sorts of tales about this place. Lurid yarns about screams in the night; weird glowings like flickering ghostly flames.

That kind of talk didn't trouble Emmy overmuch. Maybe there were ghosts; maybe there weren't, but she'd never heard tell of a phantom harming anyone with a strong heart and a love of life. Kicking away a thick tangle of scrub weed she studied the splintered remains of a door lying flat on the ground. Then she looked up abruptly, and stared towards a crooked birch tree.

'Who's there?' she called out hoarsely. 'Are you one of my father's hands? Come where I can see you!' A moment later, she let out a piercing scream, and turned, starting to run towards where the gelding stood, ears pricked.

Someone stepped out from behind a nearby knot of twisted elder, and she screamed again, backing away. The slight figure came towards her. 'Hey, Miss Emmy, it's me. Herbie Bax. Don't be scared!'

Emmy stared accusingly at the housekeeper's fifteen year old son. 'What are you doing here?'

The youngster's face was embarrassed in the moonlight. 'Ma, she asked me to ride over ahead o' you. Quick as I could. Keep an eye on you. See you didn't come to no harm.'

Emmy folded her arms. 'I don't like being watched all the time, Herbie.'

'I got to do what ma tells me.' The boy glanced towards the crooked birch tree, starkly silhouetted in the moonlight. 'What'd you see 'cross there, Miss Emmy?'

She stared at him. 'Didn't you see him?'

'See who?'

'He was huge. Built like a barn. Staring straight at me.'

Herbie gulped. 'I didn't see nothing. But then I was kinda ... watching you, Miss Emmy.'

The girl glanced back at the tree. 'I guess it was moonlight playing tricks. It gave me quite a turn.'

'Never did like this place,' mumbled Herbie nervously.

At that moment his pony nosed from behind the clump of elder, and Emmy saw it carried no saddle. 'You must have come at quite a lick. And bareback, too. That's some riding, Herbie!'

He flushed. 'Heck. It was nothing.'

Emmy touched his arm momentarily. 'Well, I guess I'm glad you're here, Herbie. Now you can ride back with me.'

'Sure.' He grinned. 'Be a real surprise for all your pa's boys when they see us riding into the yard, won't it?'

'I guess it will,' agreed Emmy with a faint smile.

They both rode off without looking back.

It was round three in the morning, with dawn already starting to pink up the eastern sky that a single shot rang out over the silent streets of the town called Victory. Plenty of people heard it, as they lay sleepless in the sweltering heat. Nobody paid too much attention. Someone loosing off a shot at a prowling wolf, maybe, or blasting a hole in the head of some skulking, verminous coyote. Nothing to worry about.

THREE

A lone horseman rode into Victory around nine the next morning. The sun was already high and hot, and there was plainly no rain coming today to damp down the clouds of dust he brought with him. Over the street, just opening up, the manager of Wallis' General Store found it hard to make out much about the tall stranger. Hard to tell even what age he might be, he was so muffled up in a clinging coat of dust. He swung off his mount and looped the reins over the hitch-rail outside the frontage of the Jawbone Hotel. The horse just kind of sagged there, about ready to drop.

'I'll see to you presently, old friend,' muttered Buzz Broleen, wearily. The two of them had ridden a long way together the last week or so, and they both needed resting-up. He set off up the rickety steps, then turned at the top, and screwed up his eyes against the sunlight as he stared back along the street, back the way he'd come.

They would have come this same route; his mother and his father. In a tired kind of way Broleen wondered whether he might see some shadow of that moment they'd approached the scatter of buildings that would have been all that was here back then.

They'd come in some style compared to most travellers hopefully heading west to claim what was due to them by the Homestead Act. A brace of heavy laden pack horses would have led the way, chivvied on with a stick and a kick or two now and then. Following close behind would be a well-matched team, horses with big shoulders and bigger hearts, hauling a wagon loaded with household goods, rolls of barbed wire, and a plough. There'd be a handsome, sun-browned woman handling those horses. Dog-weary sure enough, but with a smile on her lips, knowing she and her man, and the child asleep in back of the wagon were almost here, almost where they'd planned to be.

There was no ghostly wagon, no phantom pack horses coming out of the dust. Just a couple of dogs running and snapping at each other. Buzz Broleen flicked off a troublesome fly, shrugged all the memories away, and carried on into the hotel lobby. It was stuffy with the reek of old tobacco fumes. In his time he'd seen plenty of hotel lobbies like this. He could likely walk blindfold through it, sliding past the shabby leather-upholstered rockers, and the brass spittoons, their brightness dulled by neglect.

The clerk behind the desk was flipping the pages of a tattered magazine. He was a short, skinny youth, weasel-faced, with close cropped sandy hair. There was a dog-eared register near him, held open by a squat bottle of ink. Looking up he eyed the newcomer with bored indifference, not even bothering to bare his smoke-stained teeth in the semblance of a smile. He didn't own this run-down place, and he got paid less than he dreamed he was worth, and he just didn't give a Mexican's spit about anyone or anything.

'You got any rooms?'

The clerk wrinkled his nostrils, 'You seen the sign outside, mister. This here's a hotel. What else we gonna have here ... mountains?'

Broleen took off his hat, and slammed it down on the counter, sending trail dust everywhere, and the clerk jumped back like he'd been shot. 'Hell, why'd you do that?'

'I asked you a question.'

As the clerk met Broleen's steady gaze, his manner and his mood changed some. He saw a light there which told him that this man was not some broken-winded saddlebum you fooled with. His eyes slithered to the hefty .44 strapped at the customer's hip. You couldn't buy a walnut butt that smooth, that polished. That kind of shine only came with use. A lot of use.

'Sure we got rooms!' he declared hastily. 'Any room you like, mister....'

'Broleen. Room and a bath?'

The clerk scratched agitatedly at one of his sandy eyebrows. 'I'm sorry, Mr Broleen. No bath. You can have a real big jug.'

'Big enough to soak myself in?' growled Broleen.

The clerk giggled nervously, like a girl. 'You see how it is round here, mister. We ain't had a drought like this for more'n ten years. We just ain't got the water to spare. Even got ourselves a town ordinance about not wasting water.'

Broleen stepped back a pace or two. 'If that's how it is, that's how it is. No bath, then. So what did you charge for a room last year? Two dollars a night?'

'Last year?' The clerk hesitated, then shrugged. 'Sure. Two dollars.'

'You put your prices up since then?'

'No, sir. Good value, I'd say.' He looked pleased with himself. If he could get this one to pay two dollars then he'd be fifty cents to the good.

Broleen sucked in his breath. 'You have a drought last year?'

'No sir. Rain was late-coming, sure. But like I say, this is the worst we've known since....'

'So last year I'd have been able to soak in a brimming tub?'

The clerk suddenly realised what was coming, and saw his fifty cent profit soak away into the dirt. 'I guess we'd better say a dollar fifty, then, on account of there being no bath.'

'I'd sooner say a dollar.'

'Listen, mister,' whined the clerk in alarm. 'I don't manage things round here.'

'I figured that.' Broleen dropped the coin on the counter. 'I'll just pay for one night for now.'

'Mr Wallis ain't gonna like it!'

'The boss?' The clerk nodded. 'Jude Wallis, would that be?'

'You know him? Well, if he's a pal of yours....'

'Nope. Never met him. Well, not so I'd recall, anyhow.' He slapped some dust off his vest. 'Now make sure I get *two* jugs of water brought up to me. And find someone to take my mount down to the livery I spotted down the street. You can do all that for me, can you?'

The clerk nodded briskly. 'Sure. You can have room number one, Mr Broleen. Top of the stairs. Biggest and best we got.'

'Got a key?'

'No sir.' He glanced at the row of empty hooks behind him. 'We did once, but....'

Broleen shrugged. 'It figures. I got nothing worth stealing, anyhow.'

'That's fine then,' gabbled the clerk. 'I'll give the girl a shout. Get her to fetch up some water for you. And I'll take your horse down to the livery myself....'

Broleen had taken two of the stairs when he turned back again, knowing the clerk was still watchng him. 'One thing.'

'Yessir?'

'Where's the Jawbone?'

The clerk gaped. 'How's that?'

'The place is called the Jawbone Hotel, isn't it?'

'Oh sure it is.'

Broleen stood there on the stairs shaking his head. 'Where is it, then? Used to stand out front. I recall seeing it when I was a kid.'

'You used to live in Victory, Mr Broleen?'

Broleen sighed, and spoke very slowly. 'Where is it now?'

'Hell, I don't know. I ain't lived here that long. Mr Wallis must of took it. You could ask him, I guess.'

He suddenly realised he was talking to empty air. Buzz Broleen had trudged on his way. The clerk scowled. Fellers like that thought they were so blasted important. Just 'cause they packed a side-arm and drifted round what was left of the frontier. Thought they were better than folks who stayed in one place all their days, like him.

'Well, he's nothing, not really,' he grumbled, and remembered he had to go look to the drifter's horse. He went into the kitchen first, though.

Trudi was sitting there drinking a cup of coffee, her skirt pulled half up to her knees. He got a quick look at those shapely legs before she covered them up, and then he glowered at her.

'You got nothing better to do than drink coffee?'

The fair-haired girl eyed him with contempt. 'I've done my chores, Radley Carmichael. More than you've done!'

'Just persuaded someone to take a room here.'

'Glory be!' she marvelled sardonically. 'Ain't you the clever one?'

She shouldn't talk to him like that. He was in charge here. Yet all he ever got from her was mockery. When she'd come to work in the kitchen he'd started to imagine that maybe the two of them could....get together, when nothing much else was happening. He'd heard tales about Trudi and what she got up to. Trouble was she was plainly getting up to those things with old Mr Wallis, and it made her real sassy with him.

'He wants some water.'

'Fine,' she retorted idly. 'I'll take him a jug up when I've finished this coffee.'

'You take up two jugs, you hear?' he blustered.

Trudi looked him up and down. 'Two? That ain't allowed.'

He faltered under her blue-eyed stare. 'Sure, I know. Just this once, it won't matter none. This Broleen feller, he's ... he's....'

She laughed, 'You're scared of him, that's what it is. Then you're well nigh scared of everything that moves. Still might be worth sliding up to take a look. Tall is he? Handsome?'

'How the hell would I know?'

She finished her coffee, and gave him a coarse

grin as she leaned back, letting her blouse stretch tight over that amply desirable bosom. 'Heck, if I like him, he can have all the jugs he wants!'

An hour later, Broleen took himself down to the eating house a few doors along from the hotel. By rights he should try getting some sleep, but he knew it wouldn't come this time of day, with the growing noise and bustle outside. There was some kind of fuss going on over at the Bank across from the hotel, with a big line building up, and plainly nobody arrived to open the place up. A lot of shouting and milling around with the growing heat making everyone testy and argumentative.

The counterman was of middling age, with a wispy moustache, and a balding head the shape of the eggs in the bowl near his hand. Cheerfully, he poured Broleen a cup of coffee and sent him over to a corner table while he set to fixing a plate of ham and eggs.

Broleen sat rolling a smoke, and grinning at the memory of that buxom girl who'd brought up the pitchers of water to his room, with a glinting promise in her blue eyes. He flicked a lucifer into life. That kind of promise generally led to trouble.

The counterman had a couple more customers to deal with now. Leaving the skillet for a moment he turned and grinned in his friendly, lopjawed way. 'What can I get you folks?'

There was a nervous hesitation about the way these two approached the counter, and watching from his table, Broleen figured they didn't bring themselves into eating places much.

No mistaking them for anything but nesters. The man wore a broad brimmed grey hat, torn at the crown, and a faded linsey shirt tucked into jeans supported by fraying suspenders. His boots were so worn that he'd have burned his feet trying to strike a match on them. The woman with him was slightly built, in a limp, washed out blue cotton dress and a pair of man's shoes, run down at the heel. They both had a parched, hungry look to them, speaking of hard times and worse to come.

'How much for a cup of coffee?' the man asked hoarsely.

The counterman thumbed back to the blackboard hanging behind him. 'Like it says there.'

'How much if you put it in a smaller cup?' That was the woman who'd spoken.

The man behind the counter shook his head. 'Heck, we only got one size mug, ma'am.'

Broleen watched expressionlessly as the man dug deep in the pocket of his jeans, brought out a coin or two, and then dug still deeper. He looked at his wife, who pushed some greying strands of hair away from her face with red, work-roughened hands. 'I guess we can....'

She shook her head. 'No, Ethan. I don't need no coffee. I don't need nothing. Let's jus' go stand out in line by the bank again.'

Ethan's shoulders sagged. 'That won't do no good, neither, Sal. Mr Candell ain't going to give us no more time to pay.'

'It's the only shot we got left,' she said fiercely, and then noticed Broleen watching and listening. She grabbed her man's sleeve, her face reddening up. 'Let's get out.'

Broleen rocked back in his chair, catching the

counterman's troubled gaze. 'You slice a few more pieces of that slab of ham, slap a couple more eggs in that skillet, and fill the two biggest mugs you got with coffee for these folks.'

'No!' The woman shook her head fiercely. 'Maybe you mean well, mister. But Ethan and me never took no charity. Not from no-one!'

'Don't suppose you ever did, ma'am,' Broleen kept his tone even. 'No more than my folks ever did when they worked their holding round these parts. I'm not offering charity. Just seeking a little company. Hate eating alone. You can pay me back one day.'

Ethan shook his head. 'You'll be waiting a long time, mister.'

'I'm a real expert in waiting!' Broleen grinned. 'Just come sit down over here.'

It was the woman who decided, just as he'd known it would be. She was as proud as his own mother had been; a defiant, burning pride maybe, but hemmed round the edges with a commonsense which told her that sometimes pride might be swallowed along with a filling plate of ham and eggs.

The two 'steaders started to move towards where he sat, and then there was a clatter of bootheels on the boardwalk outside, and three men strode in, and Broleen's nose suddenly twitched at the smell of trouble. They were cowhands, he figured, angular, well-muscled; they'd also found what they were looking for, and it wasn't breakfast.

One of the new arrivals, bullet-headed, with a shapeless nose recalling some barroom brawl, swaggered straight for the man called Ethan.

Clamping a hand on the farmer's shoulder, he dragged him round. 'We been looking for you, Grice. Your boy said you'd come into town.'

The woman turned on him. 'You been to our place, Harry Crouch? If you've done anything to hurt my children....'

Crouch laughed in her face; a mocking, contemptuous laugh. 'Never touched 'em.' He jutted his spiny chin towards Ethan. 'Mr Tyler wants words with you. Little matter of a missing steer calf.'

Ethan Grice shook his head. 'What you talking about?'

Another of the cowhands had come round the other side of him. 'Some of Mr Tyler's stock drifted on your land last week, Grice. Ain't that so?'

Sal Grice pushed next to her husband. 'Drifted? They came charging onto our land 'cause somebody cut through our fencing. 'Bout a dozen of them. Trampled or ate up most of what was growing there. We drove them off.'

Crouch laughed again. 'Most of 'em, sure. But not all. We found what was left of one of them half buried.'

'That'd be a wolf done that.' There was desperation in Ethan's voice. 'We never took none of them. We never stole nothing in our lives.'

'Seems to me,' retorted Crouch, 'That it's real easy to blame a wolf for something these days. That steer'd been butchered. I never heard of no wolf using a chopping knife. Now you come on, Grice. You got questions to answer!'

Broleen had been watching all this impassively enough, but when the cowpoke's hand started to stray towards his holster, he pushed himself back from the table, and the chair squealed on the pine flooring. 'If this Tyler feller's got some charge to make, then he'd best go see the sheriff. 'Cause I see no star sparkling from your vest, mister, and that means you can't come dragging folk away from their breakfast.'

Their attention switched on to him. 'You keep outa this, stranger.'

Broleen blinked. 'I asked these folks to come sit with me.' He fired a glance towards the counterman. 'Those eggs done?'

'Sure, they're ready for eating,' came the uneasy answer.

'Then they need eating.'

The man with the squashed nose let go of Ethan's shoulder and moved a few slow steps closer to Broleen's table. 'Maybe you had something to do with this cow-stealing, too. Being as you're so close with these stinking nesters.'

He inched closer; his horny hand hovering just above the butt of his Colt.

Mrs Grice let out a little cry. 'Listen, mister. We're grateful for the offer of breakfast. But don't go getting hurt on our account. Ethan's done nothing. He'll go with Crouch here. See Mr Tyler and everything'll be fine. You see.'

There was no conviction in her voice, and Broleen shook his head. 'I've met good ranchers in my time. And bad. And the good ones don't send ugly bastards like this to do their work for them.'

A scowl fell over the cowhand's face like a dark curtain. He came on a few more steps. 'Now, mister, you is asking for something.' His menacing voice was flat as a knife-blade. By way of reply Broleen jabbed out both hands and the square edged table went skidding into the man, below the belt. It blasted every ounce of breath out of him. Crouch let out a choking howl, and staggered back, clutching at himself in agony.

Broleen was on his feet now. He hauled the gasping man round by his collar, and slammed him back against the wall, holding him with one hand, while he dragged the side-arm from the holster, and dropped it to the floor.

'I doubt you've got much down there, mister, but let's hope it hasn't squashed as flat as that nozzle of yours. 'Cause you'll be even more of a disappointment to the ladies than you are already.'

He stepped back, and Harry Crouch hunched there still grunting and moaning. 'Now you and your pals get outa here. My breakfast is getting cold.'

The other men had been watching carefully, weighing things up. One of them shrugged. 'Come on Harry, let's git. This can wait.'

As Crouch, still bent over, hobbled to the door, he turned and gave Broleen a blistering stare. 'We'll fix you good!' he croaked.

Ignoring him, Broleen pulled the table back to where it had been, and straightened the cloth out. 'Now then, you folk come sit down, and tell me just what's going on round this dusty little town.'

Sal Grice slumped into a chair. 'We ain't heard the end of this. I know we haven't. If Deal Tyler wants rid of us then things is going to get even tougher. We figured he'd leave us be, but I guess if we're in his way....' She shook her head. 'But we didn't take that steer, I swear, whatever Harry Crouch said.'

Ethan tugged at his shirt as he brought a chair round. His face was grey with worry-lines. 'None of it makes a whole lotta difference in the end,' he mumbled. 'What with the drought and all. We can't grow crops, we don't make no money. Old man Wallis won't give us no credit at none of his stores so we don't eat 'nough to keep alive hardly.'

His wife watched him impassively. 'And we can't pay what we owe Mr Candell at the bank, neither. When it comes to it Ethan's right. Tyler can't do nothing worse to us than the world and the weather's done already.'

'Breakfast coming up!'

The bald-headed counterman came over, somehow balancing three hefty plates at once, and Broleen watched the faces of his two companions as the food was set before them, and knew they hadn't eaten as much grub as this in one go for a good few months. Talking could come later, right now, they all just needed to eat.

When the talking did come, he didn't learn much he hadn't guessed already. They'd been in Brady County close on ten years. Soon as life was starting to run a little easier, the drought came along to burn up everything they'd been putting together for them and their four children.

'Josie, our youngest, she's five years old.' Sal Grice mopped up the last traces of grease on her plate. 'Mary and Ellen, they're twins.'

'Heading for fifteen,' said Ethan proudly, 'Real pretty girls.'

'So they are,' agreed his wife. 'And our eldest boy Matt, he's just turned seventeen.'

'And I jus' hope young Matt kept his lip buttoned when Harry Crouch come round looking for me,' fretted Ethan. 'He's got a temper that one.'

'He's got sense, too,' cut in his wife, and looked at Broleen. 'Maybe I should of stayed at home, but I figured I better come see Mr Candell too. Ethan here can get his tongue in a real tangle.'

Her husband shook his head sorrowfully. 'That's true, Mr Broleen. Sometimes my Sal here's a better man than I am. We had this trouble at the general store a while back, and she gave Mr Wallis a real tongue-whipping over that.'

'We was being cheated!' declared Sal, and she prodded Ethan in the arm. 'But you ain't to talk so, Ethan Grice. Wouldn't of stayed with you all these years if you'd been made of milk'n water. But Willy Candell needs telling. You can't get blood out of a stone, and stones is about all we got left right now.'

Broleen rolled himself another smoke, and thought about his own parents, and how things had gone wrong for them. But he didn't figure telling the tale would make the Grices any easier in their minds. Instead, he asked, 'What'll you do if he won't let you hold off making payments till matters improve?'

Ethan's jaw tightened. 'Guess we'll just wait for him to come take the farm over. And being as there's maybe twenty, thirty families like us, he'll have his work cut out.'

Smoke drifted slowly round Broleen as he considered that one. That was feeble hope talking. There'd be plenty of men willing to earn an extra dollar or two to drive the defaulting nesters out. He'd seen this happen before, down in Kansas, where a group of desperate 'steaders put up a fight, and ended up watering the land with their own blood.

He said nothing of this either. He wouldn't be telling them anything they didn't know already, deep down, and ripping away the bandage of hope they'd wrapped round themselves would be like dropping salt in an open wound.

'Anyhow,' said Ethan. 'We're real grateful for this chow, Mr Broleen. And one way or 'nother we'll make sure we pay you back one day. Ain't that so, Sal?'

'It sure is,' she said firmly, as she stood up. 'Real Christian of you, Mr Broleen. If you're round our way any time, you come see us, you hear. Our place is other side of Hogtail Ridge. You know it?'

'Close to Jawbone Flat, that'd be?'

'That's it,' said Ethan. 'Heck, I get to wondering sometimes if'n we should go prospecting up there. Still stories that those rocks is bulging with silver ore.'

'Yeah,' recalled Broleen, 'I heard my father talk 'bout those stories.'

'And that's all they ever was,' Sal Grice cut in. 'Stories. And dreams like that ain't gonna help us none, Ethan. Anyhow, Mr Broleen, we ain't got much, but you'd be welcome to share a bite with us.'

'Real welcome,' confirmed her husband.

Broleen nodded. All these thanks for a couple of plates of breakfast made him uneasy, but you couldn't brush gratitude away, when it was all they had to give. 'I don't know for sure how long I'm staying round these parts.'

Sal eyed him thoughtfully. 'We spent so much time talking 'bout ourselves, Mr Broleen, we never did ask nothing about you.'

'Nothing to know!' He got to his own feet. Casually, he said, 'I'll take a walk out with you.'

Things had hotted up still more outside the Loan and Savings Bank. It seemed that half the population of the town was gathered there now, noisily speculating about why Willy Candell hadn't opened up. Ethan and Sal quickly found someone they knew; a bony young man with haunted eyes, plainly here for the same reason as them.

He looked curiously at Broleen, as he told his friends what he knew. 'They say he's run off. Bank all locked up and no sign of him. That long-faced cashier doesn't have no key. Said Willy Candell kept promising to give him one, but never got round....'

Sal butted in, 'Reckon he's run off taking all the money?'

'No. It ain't like that,' asserted the young man. 'It ain't his own bank, for all he acts like it is. And it seems there's two fellers on their way over from Head Office today to look at the books.'

'They'll likely have a key for the door then.'

The young man nodded eagerly. 'Heck, Sal. Seems they'll have keys to everything there is. Real important fellers. Cashier went over to Blue Valley Junction a while back to meet 'em off of the train. They'll be here real soon.'

'Seems like Candell's been milking the cow on his own account, then,' mused Broleen. 'Decided to quit before they find out.'

A sudden raucous cheer went up. 'Hey, they're coming. The bank fellers are coming!'

For the next few minutes it all turned into quite a carnival, as the flush-faced cashier steered the buggy through the crush of interested spectators. If his passengers, two dark-dressed city types, were unsettled by having such a welcoming committee, they didn't show it. They might have been carved out of granite for all the reaction they showed.

Buzz Broleen took a walk round the bank building while the procession approached. Just one window round the side; probably Candell's office, with the blind pulled down tight, and no way to see in. He paced back to the front and bided his time close to the door, just an idle watcher on the surface, but with a whole lot of emotions churning round inside.

The buggy finally got to its destination, and Candell's cashier led the two grim men towards the door. One of them addressed the crowd. 'No point in anyone staying round today. Bank won't be open for business. Not till tomorrow.'

Nobody moved. They weren't going to miss the opening of the door they'd been staring at for the last two hours or more. Still, they kept a respectful distance. Broleen, seemingly unnoticed, just stayed where he was.

A bunch of keys appeared in one of the men's hands, and he tried a few before finding the right one. He and his colleague disappeared inside, leaving the cashier standing in the doorway like some sort of sentry. No more than a second or two passed, when one of them appeared back again. That granite expression had gone; and he was white and shaking. He stared at the alarmed cashier. 'You'd better go fetch the sheriff,' he said in a low voice.

In that stunned moment, when nobody quite

knew what was happening, Broleen stepped sharply past the man from head office, and into the bank.

'Hey, you can't go in there.'

Ignoring the protest, he headed towards the open door at the far side. The other dark-suited man was leaning against the wall by the door, plainly trying to stop his breakfast from returning to the light of day. Shakily, he asked Broleen, 'You the sheriff?'

Broleen carried on into the inner office. Candell was slumped forward on the desk. His right arm hung by his side, and a Colt revolver lay on the floor. You might say Candell was face down on an open ledger; except that there was precious little of his face left. The bullet had torn through his right ear at an angle and then exploded out at the front, scattering a gruesome soup of blood, bone and brains before it.

Broleen looked at the grisly sight for a long moment with the steady gaze of a man who'd seen more than his fair share of violent death. Calmly he rolled himself a cigarette, then stepped out of the office.

'Yup, he's dead,' he announced laconically.

'Who the hell are you, mister?' The bank employee had moved to close the outer door on the hubbub outside.

'Name's Broleen. You figure he killed himself?'

'What else?' The man caught his breath. 'Never expected to find something like that.' He swallowed hard. 'Listen, I asked, who are you? You've got no right to be in here.'

Broleen lit his smoke. 'May as well stay now I'm here. Keep you company till the law gets here.'

Halfway to Hell

The other man was in no mood to protest about that. With fumbling hands he found a small cigar and tried to light it.

Broleen helped him out. 'I never met the man before,' he murmured reflectively. 'Never seen his face. Never will, now, I guess.'

The bank man started to look towards Candell's office, then thought better of it. 'It's a hell of a way to die. Not one I'd choose.'

'Not the first to choose that way. It's quick.' Broleen spoke viciously. 'A way out of your troubles. And Candell there drove more than one man down the same road. Difference is, he won't be missed.'

He paused for a long, lingering moment. 'My father had dealings with Willy Candell. So did my mother. She never got over what Candell forced her to do.'

He flicked ash on the floor, and spat on it. 'Well, maybe Candell's saved me a job.'

FOUR

Willy Candell was wrapped in a blanket, ferried over to Fisher Maclaine's funeral parlour, and was taken out and buried the same afternoon. That was how it had to be in this kind of heat. Fisher Maclaine mumbled a few gloomy words as the cheap casket was hustled into the ground, since nobody else could be found to do the job. Nobody in the cheerful crowd could make out what the undertaker was saying, though the rumour went round that the sentiments didn't come from any prayer book that had ever been written.

Head office chewed on the news of Candell's passing for a while, then wired back that the cashier would be in charge of things for now. He went home to his wife and fretted about how he was going to cope with that never-ending procession of desperate customers. The dark-suited men locked the ledgers in the office, and went to book a couple of rooms at the Jawbone Hotel.

The town of Victory quietened down in the searing afternoon heat, and the Sheriff Jake Rosco unbuckled his gunbelt, put his feet on his desk, yawned, and tipped his hat over his eyes. He soon found out the truth of the old saying that the law never sleeps, as someone came up the steps and through the office door. Rosco pushed his hat back, and eyed the newcomer thoughtfully. 'I figured you'd have rode on out, Broleen.'

'That so? Why'd you figure that?'

'Found what you was looking for, didn't you?'

'What was that?' Broleen dragged a chair from by the wall and sat astride it, leaning forward on his elbows. He'd hung around in the bank until Rosco had arrived, then he'd gone back to the hotel to get some shut-eye.

'One of the bank fellers told me what you'd said. 'Bout your folks having ... dealings with Willy way back.'

'So you reckon I rode into Victory to kill Candell?'

'Seemed that way. He saved you a job, and saved me arresting you for murder.' Rosco scratched his chin, and yawned. 'This business 'twixt Candell and your folks. Must of been a long while back. You taken your time getting here.'

Broleen hooked out his tobacco, and slowly built himself a smoke. 'My mother passed on just a couple of months back, sheriff. Wasn't till just before she died that she told me about Candell.'

That made it all sound real easy. One day she was alive, the next she wasn't. Nothing was that easy. Martha Broleen had been a long time dying; and he'd only been there to see the candle-end of all that suffering.

His sister Vera was weary and drained from watching it happen, from coping with it all along with bringing up three small children. For the final weeks of her life their mother had been looked

Halfway to Hell

after in the neat, white-painted hospital at the river end of the little Ohio township. Run by a charity, maybe, with volunteer nurses for the most part, but they had taken good care of Martha Broleen.

He'd walked there with Vera. 'She's weaker every day, Buzz,' his sister said, linking arms with him. 'But she's still Mother. And she's been fretting so about seeing you. I just thank the lord my letters finally caught up with you.'

Now Broleen stepped away from the memory and looked at the sheriff. 'Candell deserved to die.' A tremor went through him as he lit his cigarette. 'Though I'd sooner it'd been a touch slower, and a lot more painful.'

The sheriff sensed that was all he was going to get on that subject. He stretched, and stood up. 'You want some coffee? Hell, I know it's too hot for coffee, but it hides the taste of the water.' He went through into a small cubby-hole where the pot bubbled on a small stove, and filled two tin mugs.

'Thanks.' Broleen turned the chair right-way round, and stretched his long legs out in front of him. 'I'd say you've got a town on the edge of trouble here, Rosco. Unless you get some rain soon. Like hot fat on a stove, waiting to boil over.'

The lawman sat back down behind his desk. 'Yeah, I heard how you ran up against Harry Crouch. Ray at the eating house told me 'bout it. Seems you can handle yourself, mister.'

Broleen sipped at the scalding coffee. 'I don't figure Ethan Grice, nor his wife, for cow-stealers. But too much grumbling and grousing and you got a bloody range war on your hands.'

'And I don't need that,' grunted Rosco. 'I'll have

words with Deal Tyler. Tell him to keep his temper in check. But I ain't seen signs of too much trouble. Just too damned hot for that.'

He paused. 'Though if you're planning on staying round, just watch out for Crouch. He's a crazy bastard. Mean, too.' His eyes flicked to Broleen's holster. 'I guess you handled meaner, though. In your time.'

'I don't go looking for trouble,' snapped Broleen edgily.

'Never said you did.'

'But I hear you had real trouble in Victory, last time you had a bad drought.' Broleen watched the sheriff carefully. He figured Jake Rosco for an honest enough man. He'd met crooked lawmen in his time, and this wasn't one.

Rosco damped a finger and rubbed at the star on his vest. 'Long time ago, that was. I was down in Nebraska, eating trail-dust. Been the lawman here for couple of years, that's all. It'd be round that time that your folks ...'

'Round that time, sure.'

The lawman shrugged. 'I don't know much what went on. Same kind of trouble we got now. Dried-up creeks, cattle dying, crops failing. Hard times.'

Broleen nodded. 'Cabins catching fire?'

The lawman drank too deep from his mug and scorched his tongue. 'Sure. You get a lotta fires in a drought. You talking 'bout Polanski's cabin out on Jawbone Flat?'

'I was only a kid when it happened. My folks were real sorry about it.'

There was a hint of suspicion in the way the lawman studied him. 'You ain't the first to ask me 'bout all that. Miss Scales come to see me a few days back. Asked if I had any kind of records of that time.'

'Who's Miss Scales?'

'Benton Scales girl. He runs the Hanging B spread out Blue Valley Way. Emmy, they call her. Real pretty.'

'What you tell her?'

'Just what I told you. I don't know nothing. I ain't got records for what happened last year, never mind sixteen years back.'

'And why's this girl asking questions?'

'Maybe you should ask her, Broleen. And why are you asking these questions?'

Broleen stretched forward, and put the mug on Rosco's desk. 'I got just one more for you. About Willy Candell. You sure he shot himself?'

Rosco rubbed his burned tongue on his top lip. 'No, Broleen. I figure he hung himself! What in hell kind of fool question is that?'

Broleen stood up. 'On the edge of the desk, where the blood had dripped over. Someone had touched it. Marks of three fingers there.'

'I didn't see no finger marks.'

'And I don't suppose you will now,' said Broleen, 'Daresay everything's been scrubbed up.'

'On the desk you say? Maybe it was Candell's hand. Reaching out as he was dying.'

The other man shook his head. 'No. It was like someone had been standing there, like this....' Stepping forward, he pressed his hand on the lawman's desk. 'From the size of the marks, he was a big feller, I'd say. Bigger'n me. Or you. Standing there, looking down at Candell.'

'Look, Broleen, it ain't possible that anyone else

was in that bank!' protested the sheriff. 'Door was locked from the inside. We found the key in Candell's pocket. You must of made a mistake.'

'Guess so,' agreed Broleen casually, and he began to turn away.

Rosco was on his feet now, coming round the desk. He grabbed Broleen's sleeve. 'Now listen, you keep your lip buttoned on this, mister. I don't want folk in this town thinking that....'

Broleen swung back. 'Thinking what, sheriff?'

Rosco stepped away. 'It's just crazy, Broleen. You must of made a mistake.' He stared uneasily, 'That's how it is, ain't it?'

'Eyes playing tricks on me?' Broleen nodded. 'I guess I was pretty tired.'

'Sure you were.' The sheriff seemed to glow with relief. 'That's how it was. Candell's dead. Nothing else matters. Dead'n gone.'

'Like Professor Polanski?'

Rosco waved a hand, 'Sure.'

'And Abel Cray? I hear he was a big man. Bigger than most.'

'Now listen here, Broleen!'

But Broleen was out of the door of the office as the words died away on Rosco's lips. Turning back to his desk, the lawman moistened his throbbing tongue again, and gave an apprehensive shake of his head. Then there was a nervous cough from behind him. Startled, he twisted round, and saw Radley Carmichael, the clerk from the Jawbone, standing there. 'What do you want?'

Carmichael flapped a piece of paper at him. 'I just brung over the list of who we got staying. Three of 'em tonight.'

The sheriff glowered. 'You think I don't know

that? Broleen, who just went out of here, and the two guys from the bank.'

The clerk hesitated. 'Sure, but you told me to bring you a list whenever....'

Rosco snatched the paper from the youth's hand, crumpled it up, and tossed it away. 'Just git outa here and stop wasting my time, boy.'

'Sure, Mr Rosco, I'm going.'

Carmichael came back out into the glaring sun, and grinned slyly to himself. Maybe he was stupid, but he wasn't deaf, and what he'd just heard as he stood outside the sheriff's open door had been real interesting. He reckoned that even Trudi would listen to him when he told her what he'd just found out.

Wade Wallis eased himself down from his horse, and the yard-boy took the reins and led the animal away. 'You make sure you rub him down good, you hear!' he called after the youngster, then made his unsteady way into the house.

His father was just finishing off his supper, wiping gravy from his stubbled chin. Wade tried to keep the contempt from showing in his face. Everyone said that Jude Wallis was going downhill fast, and they'd be saying it even louder if they saw him like this.

'Why didn't you come back for supper?' grumbled Wallis. 'Hate to eat alone.'

Wade sat on the other side of the table. 'This heat takes a man's appetite away.'

'For food maybe,' grunted his father. 'Not for whisky, seemingly. You been drinking.'

'Keeping an eye on my inheritance, maybe.' Wade scowled. 'I don't trust that barkeep, pa. Be no surprise if I found out he was lining his own pocket book with some of the takings.'

'Gil Coker's no worse'n anyone else,' muttered Wallis. 'And if you're so fretted by that kind o' thing maybe you could help out more.'

'Bartending?' Wade's scowl deepened. 'That's no kind of job for me.'

'Beats me what kind of job would suit you. Hell, I spent thirty years serving in my own store. Doing that's below you, too.'

'I've done it when I've needed to.'

'Sure, and made a real hog's-ear of it last time, I recall. Arguing with that farmer 'bout whether those beans was bad or not.'

Wade looked at his father malevolently. 'I figured they was good enough for the likes of him. And that wife of his didn't have no right to bring 'em over here to show you.' The memory still griped at him. Because of that straw-sucking nester and his sour-faced woman he'd got a bawling out from his father in front of a crowd of customers.

'Those beans was rotten!' said Wallis. 'I couldn't give a buffalo's fart for the nesters. But if they're paying then they don't get bad goods. Not from me!'

He shrugged. 'Anyhow, no sense in talking 'bout that. Busy, was it, in George's?'

Wade let the memory of his humiliation fade to the back of his mind for now. He shook his head idly. 'Nobody crying into their glasses over Willy Candell, that's for sure. The two fellers over from the bank head office was in there a while. First off, they said they couldn't say nothing about Willy....'

His mouth twisted in a sneering grin. The two

city-garbed men plainly didn't get much excitement in their lives, and their fame had kind of gone to their heads. Once they'd been bought a few drinks, their tongues wouldn't stop wagging. After an hour or so there wasn't much that the customers in George's Bar didn't know about Willy Candell's crooked banking activities.

Jude Wallis listened gloomily. 'No surprise to me. Willy never had no need to blow his head off, though. Should of rode outa town before he got found out.'

'That's the American way, I guess,' observed Wade sarcastically, then hoisted out a cigar, slouching back. 'After the bank fellers had staggered back to the Jawbone, Radley Carmichael came in for a while.'

'The hell he did!' Wallis banged an angry hand on the table, and sent a greasy fork clattering onto the floor. 'I don't pay him to sit in saloons.'

'If I ran things I wouldn't hire him. I doubt I'd keep on with the hotel at all.'

'Well, you ain't running things,' snapped his father. 'Good times'll come again. Victory'll start growing, then that hotel it'll be a real gold-mine.'

Wade had heard all that before. He didn't believe it, but this wasn't the track he was meaning to ride down. 'Carmichael was telling how he'd heard something. Over at the sheriff's. Seems this Broleen feller had some beef against Candell. From way back. He got himself into the bank just after they found the body. Seems he saw a hand print in the blood on Candell's desk.'

'There'd be a real mess of blood, I guess.'

'You ain't listening, pa. The door was locked, and Willy had the key in his pocket.' He paused.

'But it looked to Broleen like maybe someone else had been in that office when the trigger was pulled.'

Wallis glowered uneasily. 'Must of been seeing things, then. Else Carmichael was hearing things. And that's just as likely. Got the brains of a mosquito, that one.'

His son ignored him. 'The hand that made the print 'longed to a real big feller. That's what Broleen reckoned.' Wade smiled, slow and malicious. 'You was telling me about Abel Cray, pa. He was built like a brick barn, I guess. Hands like hams, maybe. Being a blacksmith.'

'What in hell are you jabbering about, boy?' Wallis blasted out. 'Abel Cray died years back. What's he got to do with it?'

Flicking ash into a nearby dish, Wade went on, 'Couple of fellers in the bar started recalling how yesterday was the anniversary of the fire at Polanski's.'

'So?'

'Seems Cray always vowed he'd get Willy one day.' Abruptly he stood up. 'Hell, I know it's crazy. Just old men talking out of the bottom of a whisky glass. But how's someone flesh and blood going to walk in through a locked door, and out again?'

Wallis spluttered, 'And how's some ... ghost going to leave himself a hand print? Talk sense, Wade.'

Wade yawned noisily. 'Just telling you what's being said up town, pa. I'm going to snatch some shut-eye now.'

'You come back here! I got things to ask you!' His son had gone, though, and Wallis slumped despondently in his chair. He'd said it yesterday, the past was best left buried. First there was Emmy Scales poking around, like someone trying to dredge up weeds from a stagnant fishing hole, and now this stranger Broleen stirring the waters, too.

A chilly shiver went through him. Something was burning. He shook himself. It was only Wade's half finished cigar smouldering where he'd left it. Shooting out a pudgy hand, he dragged the dish over, stabbing the stub down until it was crushed and dead.

The remains lying there sent other old echoes ringing round his troubled head, and he stood up and went outside to stare at the moon. The stable barn was coated in dark shadow, as if a shroud had been draped over it. The horses in the corral behind it moved restlessly. Far off, a she-wolf let out a doleful bark. And Jude Wallis let out a long, rumbling sigh and wished he was twenty years younger.

Broleen sat in the shade resting his back against the blistered trunk of a crooked birch tree. Chewing reflectively on a twig, he surveyed his surroundings. Over to the north, way beyond the curving line of the creek he could see a huddle of buildings, shimmering on the horizon. That'd be the Hanging B. Half a mile to the west those hunched looking cattle, maybe fifty or sixty head, wearily trudging over the parched brown land in search of grazing would in all likelihood be some of Benton Scales's stock.

A few yards away, his horse poked and picked at the weed and scrub round the remains of Polanski's cabin here on Jawbone Flat. There were signs that there'd been a couple of other horses here in the last day or two. But there was nothing much else to see.

He had a dim memory of meeting Professor Polanski. A small, withered man, with thick-lensed eyeglasses and a flopping mass of untamed white hair. An educated man for sure, even though he had only had a slippery hold on the English language. He'd talked in that excited, arm-waving way about things a small boy didn't understand, like oppression and persecution and tyranny.

Broleen thought of his mother, then, her wasted face as white as the starched hospital bedsheets. Her voice was hoarse, maybe, but there was a strength in the words. 'Your father always said the professor had some real revolutionary ideas. Like how it was wrong for ranchers to think they owned all the land they could see. Like how it was wrong for bankers to push settlers off their land because of bad weather. Like ... like it was wrong to let children starve.'

He'd supported her head, and she'd managed to take a little water. 'He tried to help all of us. That funny little guy with snow-white hair. Him and Abel.' She sank back down onto the pillow, her eyes huge and sorrowing in her face. 'I guess I'd like to sleep now, son. Come see me again. I got something to tell you, and your sister....'

Broleen's mouth set in a thin, hard line, and he tossed the twig he'd been biting on away towards those ruins which had been made by a fiery inferno one hot summer night sixteen years ago. He could almost feel his own griping hunger, and had a clear memory of his little sister Vera burning with a fever and no money for medicine; he saw his father's gaunt, haunted face, and remembered that determined look on his mother's face that afternoon she took herself off to walk into Victory.

'I'll see if maybe I can get Mr Candell to give us a little while longer,' she'd told them. 'Maybe he'll listen to me. You stay here Reuben, and look to the children.'

She'd come back the next day, bringing food and medicine with her. Mr Candell had agreed to wait a while longer; even advanced her an extra ten dollars. A kind of sob forced itself from Broleen's throat as he remembered lying down to sleep that night and wondering if Mr Candell was some kind of saint. Anger blazed in him at the memory, and he found himself on his feet, spinning round and letting out a wild kick at the tree. 'Ten frigging dollars!' he bellowed. 'For a decent woman's honour!'

The little girl buried her face in her mother's apron while the other Grice children stood behind Sal, their faces white with disbelief and fear as one of Harry Crouch's cronies finished knotting one end of a rope round Ethan Grice's ankle.

The farmer was still dazed from the beating he'd taken some twenty minutes back. The three riders had let off a couple of shots as they rode into the yard, and he'd recognised them at once. The same men who'd come into the eating house. His left eye was half-closed, and blood from a split lip was drying where it had splashed onto the bib of his overall. They'd made him take off his boots, and now his hands were tied behind his back, and the rope tied round his ankle snaked off for about ten yards, where it had been lashed tight round a solid fence post.

Sal Grice let out a howl of contempt. 'You ain't men, you hear! I can't believe Mr Tyler told you to do this!'

Her seventeen year old son came to stand alongside her, his fists bunched by his side. 'If I had a gun, ma, I'd kill the lot of them.'

She glared at him, 'You go stand by your sisters, Matt.' There was a heart-bruising fear in her for those two pretty girls. Mary and Ellen were close to being women now, and though it was only morning these men were wild drunk.

Harry Crouch, leaning against the rough barn with a rifle crooked idly in his arm, responded to the boy's threat with a callous, drunken laugh. 'You nesters need teaching a lesson, that's what. Just think yourself lucky we ain't burned your shack down.'

Sal didn't turn to look at the cabin. She hadn't been inside since Crouch's pals had been in there. The noise of smashing crockery, and splintering wood had told its own terrible story. These men had wrecked the home she and Ethan had fought to build up over so many hard years. But they could build it up again, if they were both still alive.

Her husband looked over at her, his battered face showing a light of hopelessness she hadn't seen before even in the hardest times. He was helpless, like a tethered beast, and he felt ashamed, and that was the worst of it.

'Time for you to give us some entertainment, nester!' Casually, Crouch raised his rifle, pistol fashion, and blasted off a shot in Ethan's direction. The slug hit the ground just a short distance from the farmer's feet. Then the other men followed Crouch's example; sending a volley of shots round Ethan. He didn't move an inch; just kept his head held high, and looked with a defiant pride towards his wife and children.

Sal couldn't take any more, and she flew at Crouch. She smelled the flat odour of whisky on his breath as he laughed at her. Then he swung the rifle, catching the side of her head, and sending her sprawling. 'Try that again, and we'll have the whole family dancing! I'll bet those sweet little gals could do some real pretty high-kicking for us.'

Desperately, Sal scrambled onto her knees. 'You're too drunk for this game. You'll kill him.'

'Hear that boys? Telling us we can't shoot straight now.' He jabbed the rifle in Ethan's direction. 'Hell, maybe he'll lose a toe or two, but....'

His words were drowned by the sound of a horse and rider crashing through the skimpy trees beyond the bar, and over the edging fence. Crouch's henchman had no time to dive for cover as Buzz Broleen came straight at them. The toe of his boot met the face of one of them with a sickening crunch. That man went down like a felled buffalo, and stayed down. Broleen heaved his mount to a dead stop, and was out of the saddle in the same moment. The second man was just standing there, holding his sixgun limply by his side, gaping with the shock of it. His mouth was still open when Broleen's fist slammed into it with the force of a steam hammer. He swallowed two teeth as he fell, and lay writhing there, hands pressed to his bleeding mouth.

Back on her feet, Sal Grice hurled herself at Crouch, shouldering into him, and the slug meant for Broleen went skyward. She was a small woman, but anger gave her strength and she heaved the rifle away from him. Crouch began to turn, now going for the gun at his hip. His fingers brushed the hickory butt end then Broleen cannoned against, sending him flailing back into the side of the barn.

Crouch choked as a hand closed round his neck. His eyes bulged, and as Broleen closed with him, he instinctively brought up a knee, which stabbed viciously between the other man's legs. Broleen was so fired up with fury that he hardly felt the pain, but he loosed his grip on Crouch and the cowhand sidestepped, and lashed out wildly.

The swing was too wide, doing no more than graze Broleen's cheek, and now he replied with a scorching right. His knuckles caught Crouch on the edge of his chin, then a full-fisted punch smashed into Crouch's already flattened nose. The cowhand toppled back against the barn wall, starting to crumple, but Broleen heaved him up by his shirt-front, and sent a blistering rain of blows to the other man's head and body.

Although he had caught only a glimpse of what had been going on here, the picture was clear enough. Decent, honest, hungry people, being terrorised by men who had no right to claim membership of the human race. Men with no more heart than Willy Candell.

'I'm going to beat the living shit out of you, you bastard!' Broleen spat. Keeping Crouch upright with one hand, he sent another ferocious blow into the man's face, and was just hauling back to send in another, even harder, when someone dragged him back.

'You've finished him, Mr Broleen,' he heard Ethan yell urgently. 'No sense in killing him.'

Released, Crouch slid into a sitting position, his eyes rolling in his head, a dry, rattling sound coming from lips smeared with spittle. He seemed to be trying to say something, and then slowly he fell sideways, and lay in a tangled heap.

Broleen stood there trembling, his ragged breathing loud in his head. There'd been a madness in him then, and he was mightily glad he'd been stopped from carrying on. Staring at his bloodied knuckles, he turned slowly and saw the whole Grice family gathered there, watching in a wide-eyed mixture of awe and admiration. Shakily, he said, 'Was over on Jawbone Flat when I heard gunshots. Got here as quick as I could.'

'We're obliged to you again, Mr Broleen,' said Ethan haltingly. He rubbed his wrists where the rope had burned them. 'But we can't expect you to come by every time.'

'Then we'd best see this doesn't happen again,' declared Broleen. 'I'll get these fellers back to town, and locked up. And I'd say Deal Tyler has some explaining to do.'

Ethan shook his head. 'Maybe he does. But won't change the fact that he wants us outa here. Bank'll want us outa here.' His wife started to say something, but he waved her quiet. 'I got treated like hog-dirt today, Mr Broleen. And my kin, too. We ain't the only ones this kind o' thing's happened to. And it's gonna stop!'

Sal burst out, 'Ethan, what're you talking about?'

'I been talking to some of the other fellers, Sal. Everyone wants us out. But we ain't gonna go.' His eyes blazed. 'If this scum ...' He pointed a long finger at Crouch, who was starting to come round. 'If this scum want a fight, then they got it.'

Broleen let out a breath. 'They're stronger than you, Ethan. There's more of them.'

Ethan laughed, showing crooked teeth. There was a fiery sense of purpose about him. 'Maybe they said that about the Indians once, Mr Broleen. Look where they are now. It's war. That's what it is. War!'

FIVE

Jake Rosco had nothing against women, but he'd never felt the need to stake his claim on one in particular. He glanced at the girl riding alongside him. Hair as black as a crow's wing, with flashing dark eyes, and a tilted nose, she was a sight to tingle a man's blood on a hot and dusty morning. Maybe it would have turned out otherwise, he reflected, if he'd come across Emmy Scales when he was younger.

They'd met up on the main trail about twenty minutes before, both set on calling at Deal Tyler's Crossed T ranch. They'd joined forces, moving south of the curling ridge known as the Hogtail, and onto Tyler's land. Keeping his eyes on the trail ahead he commented uneasily, 'I got to say it, Miss Scales, you'd of done well to keep quiet about what you seen out at Jawbone Flat the other night.'

She showed her white, even teeth in a wide smile. 'All I saw were shadows in the moonlight, sheriff.'

'A shadow that looked like a real big feller. That's what everyone's saying!'

'I suppose that must be young Herbie Bax's doing,' she surmised. 'It sure wasn't me spread the story round.'

'Don't matter who it was,' he grumbled. 'Fact is, it was the night Willy Candell shot himself. And the tale spread quicker'n a dose....' He checked himself. 'Real fast.'

'You mean it spread faster than a dose of pox round a railhead camp, don't you, sheriff? Isn't that how the saying goes?' There was grim amusement in her dark eyes, 'And now they think you ought to arrest Abel Cray for the murder? Because of the fingerprints that stranger saw on the desk?'

'It's this heat,' declared Rosco fiercely. 'Addles folks' brains. Abel Cray died sixteen years ago.'

'But there's a story that it wasn't really him they buried. That he's been biding his time to get his revenge.'

Rosco bit back a curse. If he'd heard that tale once he'd heard it a dozen times. Tugging on the reins he hauled his placid mount to a stop. 'There was nobody in that office with Candell. No more than you saw anyone on Jawbone Flat.'

He breathed a weary sigh. 'Willy Candell just couldn't face spending three, maybe five years in the state pen for the cheating he'd been doing. He wasn't murdered by no-one, human being or ghost.'

'I never said he was,' returned Emmy sweetly.

'Maybe you didn't. But I'd be obliged if you'd quit stirring up old memories. There's enough trouble simmering without adding that to the pot.'

He tapped his heels against the horse's flanks and the animal moved off obediently. Emmy kept up with him. 'All I'm trying to do is make a true history of times gone by, sheriff. And you must admit there is some mystery about the fire at Polanski's cabin.'

'I don't admit nothing of the kind,' Rosco snapped back. 'In a dry season you get a hundred cabins burning down.'

'But people generally escape don't they?' she asked. 'And nobody got out of that one. Not Polanski. Not his wife and daughter. Nor Abel Cray and Charlotte Tyler.'

'Maybe they was asleep. Smoke gets you as quick as fire. You got enough education to know that, Miss Scales.' Rosco looked at the girl again. 'And you should have enough brains to know that nobody at the Tyler place is gonna want to talk about this business. 'Cause that's why you're going there, ain't it?'

'I never told you that.' Emmy gave a haughty toss of her head, and rode a little way ahead of him.

Rosco caught up with her. 'So why are you going, then?'

'I met Mr Tyler's sister Millie in Wallis's store a few days ago. She was admiring the dress I was wearing, and I said I'd bring her the pattern. So that's what I'm doing.'

He gave a sceptical grunt. 'Millie Tyler's fifty-eight if she's a day. She'd look real comical dressing like you do.'

'Never realised you were an expert in fashion, sheriff!'

He shrugged the sarcasm aside. 'And they say she's short of a few shingles on the roof, too.'

Emmy shook her head. 'She lives in the past some, maybe, but it's the past I'm interested in. And I guess she'll recall why Charlotte Tyler was in the cabin that night. Nobody else'll tell me. Not my father, not you. Not anyone.'

The lawman scowled. 'Listen, I want to calm Deal Tyler down. You try bringing that up and he'll get hotter'n a bunch of chilli peppers. So maybe I'd better tell you what I know, which ain't much, and that's the truth.'

'About Charlotte?'

'Seems she fell out with her daddy over how he was treating the settlers back then.'

'Trying to drive them out, like he's doing now?'

Taken aback, he asked, 'How do you mean?'

'Well, that's why you're going to the Crossed T, isn't it? Because of what happened at that homestead yesterday? About the three men you've got in your lock-up.'

Now he stared at her. 'How in hell do you know about that?'

'Couple of my father's men were in town when Harry Crouch and his friends were brought in. It seems they looked as if they'd been run down by a stampeding herd.'

'Sure, a stampeding herd name of Buzz Broleen.' Crouch and his cronies were now in the cells behind his office, too pulverised to do much more than lay on their cots and nurse their bruises. He waved a hand westward. 'It was at the Grice place. Over that away.'

What Broleen had told him about Ethan Grice's ominous words made him twitchier than a steer with heel-flies. The last thing he wanted was a full-fledged civil war breaking out in Brady County, with hard-heads like Crouch being hired by men like Tyler. But if the big rancher was set on riding down that road to war, he wasn't likely to listen to the local lawman. Men like Deal Tyler had a view of the world that didn't always mirror how the law saw things.

Emmy cut into his thoughts. 'So Charlotte thought her father was going the wrong way about things?'

He blinked, 'Sure she did. Guess she was a touch like you. Sassy. Knew it all.'

'Knew what was right?' she commented dryly.

'Maybe. Anyhow, she took herself off to see Polanski one day to warn him about some trouble her daddy was planning for a nester family, and well....' he cleared his throat, 'Abel Cray was there, and I guess she took a fancy to him.'

'How do you know this?' she demanded hotly. 'You wouldn't tell me anything.'

'Lady, thanks to you, I've had folk lining up outside my door wanting to tell me all kinds of things about Abel Cray. You just been asking the wrong people, maybe.'

She considered that, and gave a haughty toss of her head. 'No, they wouldn't tell me because I'm a woman. Too sensitive to be told such things. But Charlotte was a woman too.'

'Sure,' he conceded. 'And just as hard to handle! Tyler must of blown steam outa his ears when she says she's going to marry Cray. Rancher's daughter wedding a troublemaking blacksmith! Now is there anything else you want to know?'

Emmy didn't seem to hear the question. They were approaching a ragged stand of cottonwoods now, hemming a wide, basin-like scoop in the earth which was a watering hole in a good year. She was staring towards those sorry-looking trees. 'There's something lying on the ground, sheriff. Just beyond that last tree.'

Rosco rubbed his eyes. There was something there sure enough, mostly hidden by one of the trees. 'Bones,' he said after a moment. 'Likely a dead steer. Come looking for water and ... giving up when it found there was none.'

'I don't think it's a steer,' she countered. 'Not big enough. And ...' Her voice trembled a little. 'Lying close by. That's a man's hat, I'd say. They're bones, sure enough. Human bones.'

Rosco flicked the reins and his mount set off at a sharp canter, with Emmy following close behind. They moved quickly along the edge of the dried-up waterhole. There was nothing neat and ordered about what they found; nothing like the grinning skeleton which hung from a stand in old Doc Morton's surgery. The lawman took in the tracks of wolf and coyote amongst the scattered bones and shreds of clothing. When hungry animals set upon the remains of a man they tore, and chewed, and dragged it apart.

As he dismounted, Rosco glanced at Emmy standing there, her gelding's bridle held loosely in one hand. She was calm as Christmas Eve. 'Poor man,' she murmured. 'I wonder who he was. And how long ago did he die, do you think?'

'Won't be too long ago. No more'n a couple of days,' he speculated. 'The trail's well-used. Unlucky feller, this one. Only an hour from here over that rise and he'd have made the Crossed T.'

Emmy moved towards the trees. A moment later she picked something up. 'I found his jacket, sheriff. Part of it, anyhow.'

'Once the wolves've got what meat they can, they'll start worrying at anything else. Fighting over an old jacket!' He picked up the hat, battered, low-crowned, and his eyes narrowed. There was something familiar about this piece of headgear.

The girl hurried back, waving a small black book at him. 'This was in the pocket. Got his name written in it. It's Rufus Jepp's Bible.'

Looking at the hat again, he gave a nod of recognition. 'Rufus Jepp! Seems all his praying didn't do him much good then.'

Emmy didn't seem to get more upset now that this jumble of bones had become soneone she knew. 'But where's his old mule?' she asked suddenly. 'And all that baggage he always carried with him?'

'Well, if old Rufus lay down and died, maybe the mule skedaddled. 'Specially if there was wolves skulking round.'

She walked away from him, and suddenly stooped down again. A moment later she straightened and Rosco blinked uneasily as he saw she was holding the old preacher's skull in her hand. It didn't seem natural for a woman to be acting like this.

Her eyes met his. 'He didn't die of thirst,' she said simply.

'You a doctor or something?' he burst out.

Emmy smiled fleetingly as if he'd made some kind of joke. 'No, I'm not. Though I've made a diagnosis or two in my time.'

'What in hell does that mean?'

Without explaining those words, she merely turned the skull to face him, and he goggled as he saw the neat bullet hole drilled just above the eyeless sockets, about where old Rufus's bushy eyebrows would have been.

'Who in hell would want to shoot a travelling preacher?' He rolled a calming smoke, and snatched an answer out of somewhere. 'Someone gunned him down. Stole the mule. That's how it was.'

'I daresay you're right,' Emmy agreed. 'A cruel thing to do. He never did any harm to anyone. My father used to let him hold meetings in the ranch yard.'

'Lotta ranchers wouldn't let him anywhere near their place,' observed Rosco. 'Preaching hell-fire in that reedy voice of his.'

'He was a cowhand himself before he turned to missionary work,' replied Emmy. 'Worked for my father for a while. I guess he had a soft spot for Rufus.'

There was no more need for talking. Without being asked, Emmy helped Rosco gather up the remains, and stow them in a gunny sack. Doubtless the brethren from over in Bethel would want to come fetch him and give him a proper burying. Gently she lowered the old Bible into the sack before the sheriff tied it behind his saddle.

'A man doesn't come down to much in the end, does he?' she said softly. 'Just a few bones.'

'That's it,' he agreed.

'You think you'll ever find out who killed him?'

'I'll try,' he said. 'But 'less we find the mule stowed in someone's barn, we ain't got much to go on.'

Less than an hour later they were at the Crossed T. Deal Tyler strode out of one of the outbuildings as they rode into the yard. There wasn't much of a welcome in the way he glared at them. Their horses got better treatment, and he yelled to a young wrangler to come and see to the mounts.

As the animals were led away, Tyler gave Emmy a look which would have burned a hole in old leather. 'I been meaning to have words with your pa 'bout you, Emmeline.'

'Well, you can speak to me instead,' she said calmly, determined not to be daunted by his hostility.

'Listen, Mr Tyler,' Rosco cut in hastily, 'there's a few things I got to say first.'

'When a man's got his boot heels digging into my land he'll do things way I choose,' barked the big rancher. 'Now listen here, Emmy, I don't know what Benton's playing at. Letting you....'

'Why it's Emmeline! Real kind of you to come visiting us.' Millie Tyler had emerged from the ranchhouse and now pushed past her brother, her hands outstretched towards the younger woman.

'Millie, don't interrupt!'

His sister flapped a bony hand at him in a vague kind of way. 'You never were one for being neighbourly. These folk they've rode a long ways to see us. You let them come in outa the sun and take some tea with us.'

The ranchhouse's main sitting room was a lot more imposing than Emmy had expected. One wall was dominated by a huge fireplace, a solid construction of soot-seasoned stones. The ceiling was spanned by vast oak beams, burnished to a rich darkness by smoke and age. Carved armchairs were scattered casually round the room, as were the thickly woven Indian blankets doing duty as rugs. Along one wall was ranged a collection of flintlock muskets and rifles, old pistols and a crossed pair of army sabres.

Deal Tyler sat glowering in one of the armchairs, and Rosco slumped nervously in another while Emmy sat on a long, brocade covered settle and watched Millie busying herself in pouring tea from a silver teapot.

'I never realised you were interested in history, Mr Tyler.' As Emmy pointed to the display of weapons, Millie turned and laughed. 'Oh, those aren't my brother's. They belonged to....to Oliver Windham. My fiancé. He went off to fight for the Union, and he never came back. Those things are my little memorial to him.'

Everybody knew the story of how Miss Tyler's fiancé had died at the first Battle of Bull Run, and how she'd never looked at another man since. That wasn't going to stop Millie telling the story again, though, as she handed round the egg-shell-thin china cups.

'He looked so handsome riding off to war,' she breathed. 'The blue of his uniform matching the blue of his eyes. Never did find his body. One day I'll look out of that window and see him riding back.'

Deal Tyler glowered. 'You know full well they never found him 'cause he got blasted to eternity by a Rebel cannon!'

Millie gave her brother a vague, chiding smile, and settled in her rocking chair. 'Fiddlesticks, Deal, that's just a story. He got a blow to the head and lost his memory. That's what happened.' With the sweet serenity of someone who knows they're right, placidly she sipped her tea.

'Gets worse as she gets older!' grumbled Tyler. 'In her own world now. Won't hear a word anyone says.'

'Then maybe I could just get what I gotta say of my chest,' said Rosco. 'About what happened over at the Grice place yes'day.'

Tyler had his gaze firmly pinned to Emmy now, but he answered the sheriff. 'Nothing to do with me.'

'Crouch works for you, don't he?'

Still Tyler didn't take his eyes off Emmy, and she began to feel uneasy. 'That crazy bastard ain't worked for me for near on a month now,' snapped Tyler. 'Beat one of the other hands to a pulp in a fight. Always coming to me and saying how he could clear the nesters off of my land like he did for other bosses he worked for.'

'So who is he working for, then?'

Tyler turned to look at Rosco at last, and Emmy felt she could breathe again. 'How the hell should I know? He's such a mean bastard maybe he's working on his own account.'

Emmy found her voice, 'So you don't want rid of the nesters, then, Mr Tyler?'

He swung back in his chair. 'Sooner they weren't there, sure. But they go, and another set take their place.'

Emmy gave a little nod. 'So, you've changed your mind about things over the years?'

Urgently Rosco interrupted, 'I figure I got what I came for, Miss Scales, just get your tea drunk down and....'

Tyler didn't let him finish. He rose to his feet, and took a few steps towards Emmy, towering above her. 'Sure. Once upon a time I thought different. Man needs space to spread his shoulders. But that was then. Things is different now.' He moved even closer, staring right down at her. 'They were bad times back then.'

'Not so good now.' Her voice quavered as she sensed the fury in the big man. 'Mr Tyler, I was only trying to get at the truth.'

He gave a hoarse laugh. 'You come here to ask Millie there, a poor addled woman, 'bout my Charlotte. Ask her about my girl and that seducing bastard what took her away and got her killed.'

His hands were knotted into huge fists at his side now, and a vein throbbed in his heavy neck. 'Cruel to Millie there, and come to that, cruel to me, too. You ask your pa how he'd feel if he lost a child. If he lost you. Ask him if he'd care to have some fancy-talking college girl raking up the ashes of another man's past!'

'Deal, you're letting your tea get all cold. Now sit right down and finish it up.' The voice of his sister broke the spell, and he turned away from Emmy and walked slowly back to his chair.

Emmy glanced at the sheriff who shrugged. Maybe he was just saying he'd told her so, or maybe he was just as relieved as her that Tyler hadn't reached down and throttled her. Because for one heart-stopping moment, she'd thought that was in his mind.

'Oliver bought this tea-pot for me, you know,' prattled Millie, oblivious to the tension throbbing in the air. 'His parting gift to me. Used to say that one day he'd take me to England. Said that tea's the only thing they ever drink there. Nothing but tea!' She giggled. 'I think he was only joshing me. What do you think, Emmeline?'

For a long moment Emmy couldn't answer.

Halfway to Hell

Despite the stifling heat a cold shiver went through her as she recalled the words Tyler had just used. *Raking the ashes of another man's past*, he'd said, which deliberate or not, was a terrible echo of what had happened that night at Polanski's cabin.

Broleen knew someone was looking down at him. The sun was shining through a jagged tear in the window-blind. If he could feel the sun then it must be after ten; he'd slept a full twelve hours.

He kept his eyes closed tight, and tensed his whole body, like a cougar about to vault onto its prey. In one fluid movement, he opened his eyes, flung back the sheet covering him, and dived to where his gunbelt hung at the end of the bed.

Trudi, the hotel maid, spun round, and still blinking against the strong sunlight, Broleen lowered the six-gun he'd yanked from its holster. The fair-haired girl gave a rolling giggle. 'Can't say I feel the need to wear anything these hot nights, neither. And that's some weapon you're packing, mister!'

He dropped the Colt onto the bed, turned his back on her as sharp as he could, and grabbed at the pillow. Then he turned back again, covering himself with it. 'What're you doing in here?'

'Just come up to make the beds. Radley never said you was still here. Guess you must be real weary after that fight you had yesterday with Harry Crouch and his pals. Every muscle aching and stiff.'

Her fingers played provocatively on the drawstring at the neck of her blouse. 'I'm real good at soothing aching muscles. Healing hands, that's what men say I've got.'

Broleen sat down on the bed, keeping himself decent with the aid of the pillow. 'You go heal someone else.'

Trudi shrugged unconcernedly. 'Well, any time you need some soothing company, you only got to ask,' she purred, and started to turn away. Then she swung around again. 'You been asking round about Polanski's cabin, I hear.'

'What of it?'

She tossed her head airily. 'Old Mr Wallis is real twitchy about you. Come to see me last night, and well ...' she winked. 'Just couldn't keep his mind on things, if you get my meaning. Kept asking me what I know about you.'

'Don't know why he's getting edgy, do you?'

'I guess you'll have to ask him that.'

'Guess I will,' said Broleen.

She took a step back towards him. 'You sure I can't plump up that pillow for you?'

'Just get outa here!' he yelled.

Trudi laughed, made a face at him, and slammed the door. Hurriedly Broleen heaved on his clothes, and looked at himself in the cracked mirror, rubbing the wiry stubble on his chin. He needed some breakfast, but he needed a shave more.

Downstairs in the lobby the clerk was making a half-hearted attempt to sweep up the place, though there was so much dust around it hardly seemed worth the effort. He tried to start up a conversation, but Broleen ignored him and went on outside. He waited while a wagon bounced past, fogging the air with dust as it went, then started to cross the rutted street towards the barber-shop.

Halfway across he became distracted by an argumentative crowd jostling outside the gunsmith's store. Telling himself it was none of his business, he was about to walk on when he saw that Ethan Grice was among those in the crowd making the most noise.

Grice wasn't the only nester there. There were half a dozen of those gaunt-faced men in their tub-faded overalls, surrounded by interested bystanders. He figured the man standing in the store doorway, with his arms folded, must be the gunsmith.

'Ain't our money as good as anybody's?' Ethan was shouting, waving a handful of dollar bills at the storekeeper. 'You gotta sell us what we want.'

'I'm telling you!' the gunsmith yelled back. 'I been told not to sell anything to you nesters.'

Broleen pushed to the front, moving alongside Ethan, noticing that the nester's son Matt was standing near him. 'What's going on?'

The nester's face showed only too clearly the results of the beating he'd received yesterday, with one eye still almost closed up, and a livid bruise on his cheek. 'Thing is, Mr Broleen, we got together enough to buy us some ammunition. Me and these fellers here.' His friends made noisy confirmation of what he was saying. 'Hell, you know how things is with us. We need ... protection.'

One of the other farmers butted in. 'From wolves and such. We got stock, too.'

Broleen looked up at the skinny gunsmith. 'What's the difficulty, mister? They're not asking for credit.'

Ethan gave a hoarse laugh. 'Credit? This here

store 'longs to old man Wallis. He wouldn't tell us the time of day for nothing.'

'Listen,' blustered the gunsmith. 'The sheriff told me not to sell nothing to no farmers. Figures they're looking for trouble.'

'Ain't us looking for trouble!' roared Ethan, and he began to advance on the storekeeper. 'You sell us what we need else we'll....'

The gunsmith backed away into his shop, closed the door, and they heard the sound of bolts being slammed across. Broleen shook his head. Well, he couldn't blame Rosco. After all, the nesters couldn't start a war without weapons and plenty of ammunition. The worry was, he might be causing even more trouble. The resentful farmers were in furious mood, and the cowhands in the crowd were already muttering darkly among themselves. And they were all packing side-arms.

He clamped a hand on Ethan's shoulder. 'You stay here, and keep your boys reined in. I'll stroll down and have a word with Rosco.'

Ethan's son gave a bitter laugh. 'And what's he gonna do, mister? He don't care about us. You saw what that bastard Crouch was doing to my pa....'

'You mind your language!' snapped Ethan.

Matt's face darkened with the injustice of it. Experience taught a man that grievances weren't righted quickly, maybe they were never put right at all. A youngster like Matt didn't think that way: if a thing was wrong, it needed putting right pronto.

Broleen looked soothingly at Ethan now. 'Just wait here, and you and your pals get your tempers damped down.' Swinging round, he faced the watching crowd. 'And you keep it cool, too.'

He got a few curses for his trouble. Right now this was still just an entertaining diversion, though, and doubtless they relished seeing Rosco send the nesters on their way. Broleen marched off. By rights Rosco should be at the gunsmith's now. A lawman should be out dealing with trouble, not sitting drinking coffee in his office.

As he mounted the steps, he called out, 'You'd best wake up, Rosco, you've got some peace-making to do....'

He stopped dead in the doorway. He saw a big, red-faced man, wearing a deputy's badge. He'd met this feller last evening when he'd delivered his three prisoners. Bob Casey, his name was, a cheerful Irishman, who talked too much. He wasn't talking much, just making a muffled noise through the gag tied round his mouth. He didn't stand up either, mainly because he was strapped to his chair by his arms and ankles.

Broleen moved straight through the office, past the deputy, and down the narrow corridor to the cells. He swore vehemently when he saw both doors gaping, and nobody inside. Harry Crouch and his cronies were gone. Leaving a string of curses in his wake, he stormed back along the passage, and into the office, where he quickly released Casey.

'How long you been like this?'

The Irishman shook his head. 'Two, maybe three hours. Sheriff's rode over to Deal Tyler's place. Went real early.'

Just after Rosco had ridden out, one of the prisoners had bellowed that there was something wrong with Harry Crouch. 'Said he was choking to death,' Casey told Broleen. 'He was lying on the cell floor, rolling round, and making this terrible din.'

'So you went into the cell, and he jumped you?'

'What was I supposed to do? Let him die?'

'Wouldn't have been much of a loss.' Broleen sat down behind Rosco's desk. 'It's the oldest trick in the book, Casey.'

'You didn't see him!' protested the deputy. 'He was pretty beat-up when you brung him in. If he'd died in there ...'

'Guess you had no choice.' Something told Broleen this man was lying. He'd seen the rope burns on Grice's wrists; when those boys tied someone they tied them good and painfully. But it had been just a moment's work for him to loosen these knots. Casey could have worked them free in a lot less than the time he claimed he'd been sitting here. Instead, he'd just stayed put, giving Crouch and his henchmen plenty of time to get away.

The fact was though that right now Bob Casey, crooked or not, was the only representative of the law in Victory. 'You got work to do, deputy. There's trouble brewing outside the gunsmith's.'

Casey looked uneasy. 'What kind of trouble?'

His answer was the loud blast of a shotgun from outside. Broleen dived for the door. 'That kind of trouble!' he yelled.

SIX

It was as quiet as the grave out here now. The crowd had melted back from the little group of nesters. Broleen walked quickly. Two panes of glass were broken in the gunsmith's window. One had been smashed by a stone thrown from outside, he reckoned, leaving a jagged hole. The other one had been shattered from inside by the blast of a shotgun, leaving just a few shards of glass hanging in the frame.

The gunsmith had emerged onto the sidewalk now, shaken by what he had done. 'It was just a warning shot,' he jabbered. 'I didn't mean to shoot him.'

Ethan Grice looked up as Broleen's shadow fell across him. His son, lying there on the rutted ground, was beyond anyone's help. Blood from the terrible wound in his neck was congealing fast in the dust. 'All Matt done was throw a pebble, Mr Broleen.' Tears were cutting a pale track through the grime on Ethan's grizzled cheeks. 'He was just a boy, Mr Broleen. What'm I gonna tell my Sal?'

Broleen had no answer for him. One of the other farmers touched his shoulder, and muttered, 'Young Matt was getting riled by all these folks making a joke of us. Just picked up a stone and threw it. Broke a window. Then he got up on the sidewalk.'

Broleen looked at him questioningly, 'What in hell's name for?'

The nester shrugged. 'I figure he was set on yelling something through the hole he made. Like Ethan says. Just a boy.'

And the gunsmith panicked, and let fly with a shotgun, thought Broleen, and he heaved a deep, sorrowful sigh. They said every war started with just one shot, and he figured that here in Brady County that first shot had just been fired.

Ethan Grice and his friends took their dead, and their sorrow and anger out of Victory, the crowd dispersed, and the gunsmith got his windows fixed. Broleen went for a shave, and then had himself a very late breakfast in Ray's place. Then, he went to the livery, checked on his horse, and chewed the fat over with the old feller who ran the place, whose wife was a full-blood Sioux.

'Over in the reservations they're saying that there won't be much snow this winter,' he told Broleen. 'Which means next year's going to be even drier.'

Winter seemed a long way off as the overheated afternoon shuffled listlessly towards evening. A light wind blew up but it didn't cool things down, just sent whirling clouds of gritty dust billowing into eyes and mouths, generally making everyone more edgy and argumentative than ever. It was an uncomfortable reminder that so far this year there hadn't been one of those furious, choking dust blizzards which came now and then.

From where he was sitting outside the saloon, Broleen saw Jake Rosco ride back into town. He saw him head straight for Fisher Maclaine's funeral parlour, and wondered about that. Then he watched him ride back to his office, and gave him ten minutes to settle in before he strolled over to pass on the day's tidings.

Rosco slumped into the chair behind his desk. 'I figure we should all move up into the mountains!' he snapped crabbily.

'No rain there either right now.'

The lawman glowered. 'Cooler, though. And with trouble coming, maybe the mountains'd be the best place to be.' He stared gloomily at the deputy's badge on the desk. "Specially now I'm the only law round here.'

'Maybe you shouldn't have fired Casey.'

'You tell me what else I was going to do with him!' Rosco retorted. 'He didn't convince me none with his story. Hell, he's dumber than a one-eared mule, but not so dumb that he'd go into Harry Crouch's cell like he said.'

'You figure they paid him off?'

'Nope.' Rosco smiled maliciously. 'They promised they'd pay him, which ain't the same thing at all. So he sat tight while they got away. He'll never see no money off of those boys. He's just lucky they didn't kill him.'

Broleen looked at the lawman with a new respect. He hadn't quite got round to working that one out for himself, but it rang true enough. Casey must be quite an optimist to think he'd ever get anything off Crouch. He sure as hell couldn't whine to anyone about not getting his money.

'Thing is,' Rosco told him, 'I would likely have let the bastards go myself after a couple of days.

Save the town the cost of feeding them. And the cost of a trial where they'd likely be let off anyhow.'

Broleen rolled a smoke. 'That's what I call log-cabin law, Rosco. Put together in a hurry. Rough and ready.'

The sheriff scowled. 'Maybe so. But it does for me. Keeps the peace, and I don't figure I can do a whole lot more than that.' Hauling out a filthy kerchief, he blotted the sweat away. 'But with the nesters all fired up, peace-keeping ain't gonna be so easy. You spare some of that tobacco?'

'Sure.' Broleen threw it across. ' 'Course, the farmers left town without the ammunition they'd come for. But they'll fight with pitchforks if need be.'

He shook his head grimly. 'They were none too happy when they found out Crouch and the others had flown the coop. Figured that was another sign that you were on the cattlemen's side.'

'I don't take sides,' growled Rosco, teasing out some strands of the rough tobacco. 'And I already told you that Crouch wasn't taking orders from Tyler when he called on the Grices.'

'What's Crouch got against them? That day in the eating house, claiming Tyler wanted to see them. Then going up to their place.'

'Like Tyler says, Crouch just got meanness in his blood. And you ain't gonna be no friend of his neither.'

Broleen shook his head. 'It doesn't much signify either way. Ethan Grice has lost his son now. An accident, maybe, but it's a death you could have done without, Rosco.'

'Like everything else boiling up round here,'

retorted the sheriff, tossing the makings back. 'Nesters on the warpath, someone murdering a travelling preacher.'

'And what did Tyler have to say 'bout that?' Broleen inquired thoughtfully.

'He didn't, 'cause I didn't ask him. I got Emmy Scales outa there soon as I could. He don't like to be reminded about his gal going off with Abel Cray. Then getting fried for her trouble.'

'No man would, I guess,' commented Broleen. 'But it sounds to me like that little lady's tough as teak.'

'And stubborn as a Missouri mule, too.'

'I never reckoned women to be soft,' muttered Broleen. 'They get it a lot harder than men. And they take it. Bringing up kids out here isn't easy. Watching them starve. Knowing there's little enough they can do about it. Suffering, and keeping going.'

'Like your ma?'

'All women,' snapped Broleen.

For a while they smoked in silence, then Rosco said, 'I still want to know why she's so plumb interested in what happened to Polanski and the others.' His eyes narrowed, 'And that goes for you, too, Broleen.'

'Maybe I'll tell you when I'm good and ready.'

'That mean you're set on staying round for a while?' asked the lawman. Broleen twitched a non-committal shoulder and Rosco went on, 'Thing is, you can handle yourself. Taking on those three over at the Grice place. Then bringing 'em in single-handed....'

'They were in no state to cause me any trouble.'

Rosco shrugged. 'Maybe. But you got a lot of

sand, mister. How's about earning yourself a few extra dollars?' Meaningfully he picked up the star he'd yanked off Bob Casey's shirt.

'You want me to sign up as a deputy?' Broleen laughed. 'Why'd I do that?'

'Ethan Grice and the others, they kinda trust you. Could help cool things down.'

'That's a reason for you, not for me,' Broleen fired back.

Rosco picked at a front tooth, worrying at a fleck of tobacco caught there. 'Well, think about it. Wouldn't be for too long.'

'Maybe that's the truth,' retorted Broleen. 'Getting caught in the crossfire between farmers and ranchers is a good way to shorten a man's life.'

Rosco's gaze didn't waver. 'Wouldn't be the first time you've done it. You been a lawman before.'

Broleen raised an eyebrow. 'Who says?'

'Those pinholes on your shirt.' He jabbed a triumphant finger. 'Just about where a man would fix a lawman's star.'

Broleen let out a long whistle. 'Maybe you're not as stupid as you look, Rosco!'

Rosco let the insult slide by him, too pleased that he'd struck at the truth. 'Just a deputy was you, or maybe more'n that?'

'Small township in Kansas,' answered Broleen after a considered pause. 'Marshal got himself killed by a gun-happy drunk. I got voted in. Not difficult since nobody else wanted the job. Only did it for a month or so, then I got a letter from my sister. Went back to see my mother, before she ... passed on.'

'Tough town?'

'I managed.' Broleen got to his feet. 'If I decide to take up your offer, sheriff, maybe I'll tell you. Right now, I got other things to do.'

The deputy's badge clattered back to the desk. Rosco grinned uncertainly. 'Well, you ain't a citizen of this fine town, so I can't force you. But you'd be a good man to have along.'

'I'll think about it.'

Broleen emerged into the dust-swirling twilight, and clapped a hand to his hat as the breeze tried to pluck it away. He moved down towards the hotel, where the lamps had already been lit in the lobby.

The clerk was talking to someone; a big, flabby man in a tired suit. Carmichael was doing his best to look respectful, but the effort was just twisting his ferret-face into more of a sneer than usual. 'It just ain't so easy to keep this place clean, Mr Wallis. Soon as you brush up one lot of dust, it just blows back in again. It's just....never-ending.'

The man at the counter heard Broleen come in. He turned his heavy-jowled, unhealthy features towards the newcomer. 'You'll be Broleen, I guess. The man who figures a dollar a night is enough for the privilege of staying here.' He spoke jerkily, waving his fat hands. 'Well, let me tell you mister. If you want to stay on here you'll pay the extra fifty cents. Starting tonight.'

He stared belligerently, and behind him, Radley Carmichael smirked. Broleen shrugged indifferently. 'Guess if that's how it is.' He fished in his pocket, and hurled some coins towards Carmichael, who ducked, letting the money clatter off behind him.

The big man scowled, but some of the hostility

had gone. He'd won his petty battle. 'You set on staying much longer?'

'Depends,' returned Broleen easily. 'I guess you must be Jude Wallis. Owner of this ... fine establishment.'

Wallis blinked at the sarcasm, but nodded. 'That's my name.'

'I was thinking of looking you up, Mr Wallis.'

The hotel owner moistened his lips, unaccountably nervous. 'Why'd that be?'

'Carmichael here told me you moved the Jawbone.' He thumbed back towards the door. 'Used to stand right outside the hotel I recall. On a sort of wooden trestle. Prof Polanski reckoned it belonged to a giant lizard or something. Used to be great herds of them roaming the plains.'

Wallis scratched his cheek. 'That's a long while back, mister.'

'Before the buffalo, sure.'

'I didn't mean that! I was talking 'bout that old jawbone.' He carried on worrying at the itch on his stubbled cheek. 'How come you got to see it?'

'I used to come take a look at it, while my folks were over at the store.'

'Who'd your folks have been, then?' asked Wallis.

'They were called Broleen, like me.'

Jude Wallis had small eyes, now they'd reduced to pin-prick size as he stared uncertainly at Broleen, trying to decide if he was being mocked in some way. 'Had the jawbone moved,' he said finally. 'Just used to get in the way of things. Ain't seen it for years. It's over at my place somewhere. Out in the stable maybe.'

'I'd sure like to see it again,' remarked Broleen

lightly. 'Prof Polanski, he was a pal of my father's. Funny little guy. Real comical seeing him and Abel Cray walking round together.'

'Your pa was a nester?' Wallis swallowed hard. 'Just what's your game, Broleen? Stirring up all this bunkum about Abel Cray.'

'I'm stirring nothing.'

'They was troublemakers those two. Polanski got throwed out of his own country for causing trouble.'

'That so?'

'And Abel Cray got it into his head he was some kinda knight in silver armour,' snapped the sweating man. 'Going round threatening folks. Did you hear that, mister? Making all kinds o' threats. Stirring up trouble.'

Broleen sensed Wallis wouldn't stand his pretence at politeness for much longer. But the man was plainly rattled, and he intended to carry on poking as long as he could. 'I heard Cray was none too keen on Willy Candell....'

'Cray's been dead a long while. Men don't clamber outa the grave. All this crazy talk is just....crazy.'

'Willy Candell *is* dead, though.'

'So's Cray, I tell you!' blustered Wallis. 'And Polanski. Used to hold meetings. Firing people with rabble-rousing talk. Like he was some kind o' preacher like....' He waved an agitated hand. 'Like old Rufus Jepp or something.'

Broleen nodded. 'Well, you won't have heard, Mr Wallis. But Rufus Jepp's dead, too. Found out in the middle of nowhere with a slug in his skull.'

Wallis flinched as if he'd been hit by a bullet himself. 'Jepp dead? Murdered?' The idea made him sweat more than ever, and Broleen knew he was looking at a frightened man. Wallis licked his lips again. 'Ah, I ain't got time to be bothered with this right now.'

Swinging round, he brandished a pudgy hand at Carmichael. 'And you just see this place gets cleaned up!'

'You'd best tell Trudi that, Mr Wallis. She don't hardly listen to nothing I say.'

'I'm telling you. You run this place for me. If you can't ride the horse then you'd best get outa the saddle.'

Without another word, he waddled out. Carmichael scowled. 'Trudi's the only critter *he* rides these days.'

Unable to raise even a flicker of sympathy for the clerk, Broleen just shrugged and went on his way upstairs. He turned into the semi-dark of his room, and closed the door. The perfume was the first thing he noticed; a flowery fragrance which could only have come from the scent bottle. In the murky half-light drifting in through the blind he saw everything else in a baffled rush. Clothes, a woman's clothes heaped on the chair by the window. Someone lying in the bed, just covered by the sheet.

Heaving in an irritated breath, he walked to the edge of the bed, looking down. 'Decided to take a lay down after tidying the bed, Trudi? Well, I'm going out for five minutes. And you'd better get yourself dressed and outa here before I come back!'

He heard a silvery laugh. 'And who, may I ask, is Trudi?'

She turned on her side, the sheet falling away

from her shoulders, and rested on her elbow. Despite the dark Broleen swore he could see that uptilted nose, those dark eyes alive with amusement. He couldn't move for a moment; frozen by the surprise and the pleasure of it.

'What're you doing here?'

Emmy Scales laughed again. 'Not pleased to see me?'

'I can't see you. It's too dark.'

'Then you'd better come a little closer, hadn't you?' she purred. 'Come on, it's a big bed. Too big for just one person!'

Weary footsteps came upstairs as the two bank officials headed for their own rooms after another long day untangling Willy Candell's imaginative accounting methods. In the lobby, Radley Carmichael had a brief, blistering row with Trudi, then took himself over to George's Bar to scowl at everyone. Main Street became a canyon of dusty darkness out of which occasional riders emerged like grey ghosts. The tinny sound of a bar-room piano playing off key drifted out from a saloon. Jake Rosco made himself some more coffee, and hopefully polished up the deputy's badge with his sleeve.

For the two people in the big bed, none of this was of much consequence. The last time Broleen had seen Emmy was over two months ago. She'd been leaning perilously out of the train window, waving wildly as she headed westward from the little Ohio town. He couldn't see her now, but he could feel her, and touch her, and the feel and the touch was even better than he remembered. There plainly wasn't much doubt that she felt the same way.

They lay still and sleepy now, he had his arm round her, and she was curled against him, her black hair brushing his shoulder. Broleen's mind went back to the first time he'd seen Emmy Scales, wearing a crisp apron, her thick hair tamed under a frilled cap. She was leaning over his mother's bed, as he and his sister came into that hospital room.

He guessed he'd been smitten by that first smile she'd given him as she'd turned to greet them. It was only later that he found out all about her from Vera.

'A lot of the girls from the college help out with the nursing. Some of them are harder workers than others. But Emmeline's one of the best. She'll do anything for anyone. And mother took to her straight off. Even before she found out Emmeline comes from Brady County....'

He felt Emmy stroke his arm. 'You're pleased to make my acquaintance again, then?' she whispered.

'I guess I am.' He ran his hand down her back. 'Though, maybe I should ... introduce myself again.'

Emmy laughed, and lay on her back, tugging the sheet up to her chin. 'I think we have to talk first, Buzz.'

'I guess. But how in hell did you get here?'

'Door's not locked,' she said.

'I don't mean that. I heard about your trip today. Finding the old preacher. Having yourself a showdown with Deal Tyler. But I didn't see you ride into town with Jake Rosco.'

Emmy lay back again. 'I didn't. Said my goodbyes to him, then took the back trail into town. My father's not expecting me home till tomorrow. Told him I was visiting an old friend in Victory.' She gave another of those tinkling laughs. 'Which is true enough.'

He eased himself out of bed, and padded over to fetch his tobacco. The bedsprings creaked in complaint as he rejoined her. 'Hell, I just hope the springs didn't make too much noise.'

'Who'd hear over the din of that piano? And who'd care?'

Broleen realised his hands were still a shade unsteady as he rolled his smoke. 'Your father wouldn't be too pleased.'

'Well,' she murmured gravely, 'you'd have two choices, Broleen, being lynched, or getting married.'

A match flared into life, and he saw her laughing face. 'Hanging's quick!'

Emmy punched him in the arm. 'Thing is you never turned up for the meeting we planned at Jawbone Flat, did you?'

'Got distracted by a little business,' he said. 'Heard these shots and....'

'The Grice homestead, I know.'

Now he told her what had happened in town today, and talking about Matt Grice getting killed like that sobered them both. 'Maybe this town has problems enough already. You and me playing crazy games isn't going to help things.'

She sat up in bed. 'It's not a game, Buzz! We're trying to get at the truth. That's what your mother wanted. Almost with her dying breath. The truth about the night Polanski's cabin burned down.'

'Sure, I know,' he mumbled.

Vera had been in that hospital room with him, and Martha Broleen had insisted that Emmy should stay. 'Me'n Reuben never had much time for your pa, Emmy. Though Benton Scales never seemed so bad as some of the ranchers in Brady County. But you've been a real friend to me....'

She was getting weaker all the time, but she wanted to tell the whole story of that time. Sometimes her voice failed her, sometimes Broleen feared that she was going to slip away before his eyes before she'd finished telling them what she had to say.

'Somehow, while Professor Polanski and Abel were on our side, we still had hope. They were kind of ... uniting us all. Abel was a big man. Had a habit of being in the right place when he was needed. The Prof was a great one for cooling tempers down.'

Emmy helped her to a sip of water. 'Then suddenly they were all dead. Burned to death in that terrible fire. And there seemed to be no hope left. So I figured I'd go to see Candell myself. I knew what kind of man he was. Knew he wouldn't resist what I'd be offering. I thought, just a little more time might help us. I went back to his house with him....'

Broleen knew he'd wish for the rest of his life that she hadn't told him everything. But she needed to. It was something she'd never told anyone. Not all of it. And she wanted to release it out of her before she passed on.

'I just told myself it wasn't happening to me. He was getting drunker and drunker. I stayed sober. Felt I had to.' His mother had held his hand painfully tight as the story spilled out.

'Afterwards, he got boastful. Boasting about how much money he made out of people like us. Then he started laughing about the Professor. I wished at that moment I had a gun, a knife, anything!'

Now bringing himself back to the present, Broleen looked at the shadow beside him. 'You recall the words my mother said. What Candell told her.'

'The gist, I guess.'

'I remember them clear as if she'd just told me,' he muttered. It was almost as if he could hear her inside his head, repeating the banker's drunken boasting: *We fixed 'em. Fixed 'em all good. Polanski and Cray, and the rest. No more trouble now they've gone. We fixed em. Me and the others.*

Then Martha Broleen had looked at her son with the kind of fire in her eyes he remembered from old times. The kind of flashing determination to make sure he did what he was told. 'All these years I've wondered if I should of said something about what I heard that night. It's haunted me ever since Reuben put an end to himself, and we came back east.'

He'd gripped her hand. 'I'll make sure him and the rest of them get what's owing to them.'

She gave a satisfied sigh, and drifted into sleep. Next day she died. In the days after that, it was Emmy who'd helped him through the first pain of grieving. Her time at the college was almost done, she'd soon be going back to Brady County, and in those days before the railroad train had taken her away, they'd got to know each other real well.

Knowing that the anniversary of the fire at Polanski's cabin was fast approaching, Emmy had come up with the plan. 'Maybe if we start a rumour going that Abel Cray's come back to get his revenge, we can smoke them out. Candell, and whoever else started that fire.'

Broleen had been doubtful. 'Who's going to believe a wild yarn like that, Emmy?'

Well, he'd been wrong, and she'd been right. Luck on her side, too. Out at Jawbone Flat that night she'd known Herbie Bax was watching her. It meant that he could spread the story about her seeing a big, mysterious man close to the cabin ruins.

She sighed, ' 'Course, I didn't know that Willy Candell was going to kill himself that same night.' She snuggled up to him again. 'But your story about the hand-print in the blood, that was really clever. Never thought you had that kind of imagination!'

'No more did I.' He shook his head. 'I saw this smudge in the blood. Could've been anything, but I just exaggerated it into a hand-print. Thing is, I'm just not sure we should go on with it, Emmy. Candell's dead. Maybe we should leave it at that.'

She ran her fingers down his chest. 'We'll talk about it again, Mr Broleen. But not now. I'd say it's time for us to get acquainted again. How does that sound?'

'Well,' he said, 'I guess your father can only hang me once!'

The light coming in through his window woke up Wade Wallis with a start. For a few moments he lay there stretching, his mouth sour with the acrid taste of last night's whisky, and then he sat bolt upright gaping at the window. The sky out there was still dark. It was nowhere near dawn, but there was a bright glow out there. He half-rolled off the bed, and moved to the open window, staring out uncertainly across the yard towards the stable building with the corral and the dark shapes of their four horses beyond it.

'Hell!' He made a grab for his clothes. The place was on fire, flames licking out through the open door, and sparks seething up from the glowing roof. He got the legs of his britches in a tangle, and almost fell over. He was about to head for the door, and wake up his pa when he saw it coming out of the stable.

First off it looked like a rolling ball of fire, moving this way and that, but then he heard the bubbling, agonised shrieking, and saw it was a man engulfed by flame. A big, lurching man with every part of him afire. It was Jude Wallis, his father, coming towards the house, howling for help, or maybe just screeching for an end to the pain.

Wade Wallis couldn't move. He stood there by the window pressing a fist against his mouth and just watched in paralysed disbelief as the human inferno stumbled ever onward. Then Jude Wallis fell; writhing there in the dusty yard, burning as bright as an overturned lamp, and shrieking like a soul in torment.

Now Wade Wallis turned away, until the din had stopped. He stared at the wall, and thought about Polanski's cabin.

SEVEN

By the time the cashier arrived to open for business, the two men from the Loan and Savings Head Office were already beavering away in the office that had been Willy Candell's. He sighed to himself. It had been a quiet few days here in the bank. There'd been a quick rush of folk taking out their deposits, thinking that they might lose them. Head office had wired through a message, though, assuring them their money was safe. The cashier had copied it out a couple of times, nailing it to the outside of the door, and tacking it on one of the inside walls. Aside from that there hadn't been much for him to do. He wasn't authorised to make loans; nor was he allowed to arrange for bad payers to be evicted.

So most everyone stayed well away from the bank, enjoying the brief freedom from worrying about financial matters. It wouldn't last long now, though. The two dark-suited men had almost finished their job; and a new man would be coming over in a few days to take over running the bank. The cashier was happy enough that they hadn't decided to promote him even if his wife was still spitting like a wild-cat about it.

'You should tell those high'n mighties at Head

Office that you've earned it. Working for Willy Candell all these years and getting no respect from him. Now you work for them and they should put you in charge. That's what you're owed!'

Her fury would run its course, he knew, so he didn't argue with her and make it worse. The man in charge of a bank got a kind of respect, sure enough, but too often that was a respect born out of fear, and underpinned by resentment and hatred. His own father had lost his livelihood when a money-lender had called in on a loan, and he didn't reckon he could ever do that to anyone.

He poked his head through the inner office door and saw there was a pile of old, dust-grimed ledgers on the desk. 'Can I fix you gents some coffee?'

Neither seemed to hear him for a moment, as they flicked through a ragged-looking account book, then one of them turned. 'Cup of coffee sounds like a fine idea.'

The cashier lingered there inquisitively. 'Some real old books you got there.'

'So we do. That cabinet over there is full of them. Seems Candell never got round to throwing anything away. These date right back almost to when he started.'

His companion gave a dry laugh. 'And he had a strange way of doing his accounts even then.'

The cashier shrugged. 'Well, that's how he was, I guess. Twisting figures to suit himself.' He paused, 'Did you fellers hear the ruckus last night?'

'What ruckus was that?'

'Jude Wallis's stable barn burned right down. And him with it.'

'Sometimes I feel so dry, I think I'll burst into flames,' commented one of the men. 'I'm looking forward to getting home and taking a real bath. A wealthy man, Mr Wallis, from what we've seen in the records.'

'All his money didn't do him much good in the end. It was quite a fire. Flames this high.' The cashier waved a hand vaguely. 'Saw most of it. His place is just a little ways from where me and the missus live.' Then he shook his head reflectively. 'Kinda queer when you think of it.'

'Why's that?' asked one of the other men.

'Well, with him and Mr Candell having so many dealings with each other, and then dying so near together. Course, Mr Wallis got burned and Mr Candell shot himself, so they didn't both go the same way.'

There was still a dark stain on the floorboards which the men from head office always avoided looking at. They didn't like to think too hard about how and where Willy Candell had died, so they cut the cashier short, and sent him off to make them some coffee. While they waited for the coffee to boil, they carried on leafing through Candell's old ledgers. They were mostly filling in time now till late afternoon, when they could ride back to Blue Valley Junction, and let the railroad take them back to civilisation.

'He was making an awful lot of loans back then,' one of them observed. 'And from the payments he was taking in, he was charging a cruel rate of interest. Look at them all. A farmer borrows a dollar and ends up paying back four, even five.'

'Or doesn't pay,' his colleague said. 'Ends up losing everything, and Candell sells the holding onto another hopeful settler, and gets that back in a few years too.'

They looked at each other, both thinking the same thing. If a man made that much money, why in hell's name would he stay out here in this God-forsaken place? They were about to close the ledger, and put it back on the pile, when one of them blurted out, 'There's something peculiar about this page. It's thicker than the rest.'

They took a closer look. 'It's two pages, pasted together. And I'd say there's another sheet of paper trapped in between these pages.'

As they set about eagerly prising apart the pasted pages, fifty yards away, Jake Rosco had the stretched, grey-skinned look of a man who'd been deprived of sleep for a large chunk of the night. He was staring disbelievingly at Buzz Broleen. 'Didn't you hear nothing? We had half the blasted town watching Jude Wallis's stable barn burn down. Even if we'd had enough water for the fire-pump I doubt it'd have made much difference.'

'Guess I slept pretty sound,' replied Broleen awkwardly. He and Emmy had woken around dawn, after all the fuss had died down he guessed. Town was quiet, nobody about, and he'd walked her back to the house where she was supposed to be staying. He'd noticed the smell of smoke in the air but had paid it no real heed.

'I figure Wallis must have been knocked out by someone before he was soaked through in kerosene and set alight. Came round to find himself and his stable ablaze.' Rosco sniffed, 'Wasn't too much left of him by the time I got there.'

'Could have been some kind of accident, maybe.'

'Sure, and maybe I'm the Queen of England!' snarled Rosco. 'If I can't get tight hold of the reins, this town is going to start galloping in all directions at once.'

He stared miserably at Broleen. 'We got one half reckoning that Abel Cray's come back from the dead to get his revenge. The other half are fixing their sights on Ethan Grice and the nesters.'

Broleen tensed. 'How come?'

The lawman rubbed at his neck. 'They had no love for Jude Wallis, did they? Overcharged 'em for everything he sold, then wouldn't give 'em credit when they ran short. And folk are starting to figure out that the same went for Willy Candell.'

'Nobody's to blame for Candell's death but Candell himself!'

The sheriff smiled thinly. 'I recall someone telling me that a big feller had been in that office, left his hand mark in the blood. Someone who had a notion that folk might start thinking that Abel Cray's come back from the dead.'

'I never quite said that Abel Cray....'

Rosco's lips tightened into a scowl. 'Didn't need to, did you? But let's say it was a more human kind of visitor Willy had that night. Ethan's lost some of the meat off him lately, but he's still big enough to fill the picture, I'd say. What'd you say to that?'

Broleen flinched under his unwavering stare, and all at once he felt his skin crawling. He'd been right to start worrying about what he and Emmy were doing. Now it looked as if their crazy story might be about to cause even more woe for the farmer and his family. He felt his heart thumping. 'Listen, sheriff....'

But Rosco interrupted. 'No, *you* listen. I ain't the world's best lawman, Broleen. Never have been. But I got a mite more than sawdust between my ears. And when I see two lovebirds floating through the shadows on Main Street round sun-up, I started thinking real hard.'

'You saw us?' exclaimed Broleen.

'Sure, I did. Mr Broleen and Benton Scales's daughter creeping out of the Jawbone Hotel in the dusty dawn. Real romantic!' Rosco's face hardened. 'She's an angel, that one. The same sweet angel what saw a ghostly figure out on Jawbone Flat. That's been going round reminding folk about Polanski and Abel Cray.'

Suddenly angry, he thumped his hand down on the desk. 'I was in Candell's office, too. I never saw no handprint in the blood. 'Cause there wasn't none, was there?'

Broleen hesitated. 'There was a kind of smudged look on the edge of the desk ...'

'Which you kinda exaggerated into the shape of a man's fingers pressing down!' bawled Rosco. 'Just tell me how it was, will you?'

'There was no handprint, sheriff.'

'So you been making a fool of me, Broleen.'

'I wasn't aiming to do that. Emmy and me, we had our reasons. Good reasons.'

Rosco gave a twisted grin. 'You're the luckiest feller in Brady County. You know that? There's fellers in this town'd give all they got just to hold that gal's hand. Hell, they'd sell their soul for a smile from her. And there's you, a spiky chinned saddlebum, getting to spend the whole night with her.'

'Spiky-chinned, maybe,' said Broleen heatedly, 'But I'm no saddlebum.'

'I don't know what you are, mister,' retorted Rosco sourly, and his grin faded. 'But 'less you start telling me just what you and that gal been playing at, then you just spent your last night cuddling up to her. You hear me?'

'Sure, I hear you, sheriff,' agreed Broleen resignedly.

Wade Wallis stretched out on the leather sofa in the room which his father had called the library. Sure enough, one wall was lined with books, but Wade doubted that anyone had ever opened the covers of most of that grotesque collection of old law and medical books, religious tracts and three volume novels his father had bought from someone over in the state capital.

'Always trying to impress, weren't you pa?' he muttered, and took another hefty slug of that fine old Scottish whisky he'd found in one of the oak cabinets in here. 'And you had a kinda impressive end!'

He laughed, lolling back. Maybe the memory of that gruesome sight out in the yard wasn't something he wanted to bring back, but it meant he was in charge now. Could do what he damn well liked.

First thing he'd do would be to get rid of that nagging old woman who came in to cook and clean and such. She'd turned up this morning weeping and wailing about poor Mr Wallis so he'd sent her off home. He'd never had got much respect from that woman, and he wasn't planning on her ever coming back to work here. He was already wondering whether Trudi might come and take her place. There'd be no work for her in the hotel once he closed that down. It'd give him a sweet sense of revenge on his pa to have her in his bed whenever he wanted.

He had other plans too. George's Bar needed spicing up for one thing. Girls with hip-high skirts and welcoming eyes and warm bodies, that's what it needed. With him taking a share in what they might earn upstairs. Lighting another fat Havana, he settled back to dream. He hadn't even closed his eyes, though, when the door of the library was shoved open. Lazily he said, 'I thought I told you to stay home today, Mrs Hicks.'

'Do I look like Mrs Hicks?'

Wallis slid into a sitting position and gave a startled stare towards the door. The man leaning there was wearing a buckskin jacket, soiled to the colour of weak coffee with sweat and grime, showing his yellowing teeth in a malignant grin.

'Door was open so we let ourselves in.' Harry Crouch's eyes were as hard as blue bottle glass. As he stepped into the room, Wallis saw the dark shadows of his two cronies looming in the hallway. Crouch took off his battered stetson and slapped it against his thigh, sending dust throbbing round the room. 'Saw the fire last night, from up on the Hogtail. Judd back there come in to see what was going on.'

One of the men behind him spoke. 'Real carnival you had here, Wallis. Could of roasted an ox if you'd had a mind.'

Crouch, his face still bruised and swollen in

places, gave a grim chuckle. 'Roasted his daddy instead. And don't he look real sorrowful, boys?'

Wallis shrugged with a calmness he wasn't sure he felt, and swung his legs off the sofa. 'I guess I'm all outa tears for him now. Taking a chance, ain't you? All of you coming back. Rosco won't be too happy to see you back in town.'

'We ain't made our presence too public,' said Crouch. 'But we figured it was a good time to come see you.'

Wallis tried to stop the flicker of nerves showing in his face. He'd never figured on seeing these men again. He'd paid them well for what they'd done for him. It was Ethan Grice who'd humiliated him that day in the store over that bag of rotted beans. Ever since then, he'd brooded about how he could get even. One day he'd heard Crouch sounding off in the saloon about how he'd helped various ranchers get troublesome nesters and squatters off their ranges. He seemed like the kind of man who'd be able to dole out a good helping of misery to Grice and his family.

'I'd have figured you'd be well away from Brady County by now,' he muttered uneasily. 'You got your money.'

'Well maybe we did. Maybe we didn't.' Thoughtfully Crouch traced the line of a livid swelling below his right eye. 'Maybe we're owed extra for the ... extra trouble we got. That bastard Broleen caught me with a lucky blow then half killed me while I was down. Micky lost two teeth.'

Wallis shook his head. 'You got paid what we agreed.'

'Oh heck, yes, sure we did,' drawled Crouch. 'But that was what we agreed when you said you was kinda short of funds. Now you can put your paw in any till you choose, and nobody to tell you otherwise.'

Stepping forward he grabbed the bottle off the table by the sofa, tipping it back and gulping a hefty swig. He passed it back to the others. 'You never did say what your beef was against Ethan Grice.'

Wallis wasn't about to tell Harry Crouch the truth on that one and risk more mockery. 'He's a nester. Ain't that enough?'

'Could be. Maybe you want us to finish the job we started?'

Wade Wallis chewed nervously on his cigar. 'How do you mean?'

'Talk is that he turned your pa into a Roman candle.'

'Someone did,' said Wallis. 'I can't figure he poured kerosene over himself and dropped a match. I guess some nester like Grice'd be as likely as any.'

Crouch was swigging from the bottle again. 'If someone done that to my daddy, I'd be madder'n a bull with bad teeth. I'd use Grice as a tree-trimming, and maybe have myself some fun with those sweet little gals of his as a kinda bonus.'

He lowered the bottle. 'And since you ain't got the belly for it, me and the boys'll help you out. Couple hundred dollars, that's all, for our time and trouble.'

Wallis gulped. 'Now hold on there. I ain't sure....'

Dropping the empty whisky bottle to the floor, Crouch pulled his gun. 'We're sure, ain't we boys?'

The men behind him gave a grunt of agreement, and he laughed. 'But we got other unfinished business, too. With a party name of Broleen. And you're gonna help us with that one, Mr Wallis.'

Wallis got unsteadily to his feet, and seemed to hear a buzzing in his ears. 'Listen, you can have all the money you want,' he jabbered. 'But I want no part of any killing, you hear.'

Casually, Crouch waved the heavy Colt at him. 'Sure. But 'less you help us, then you'll be taking a real close part in a killing. Your own. You'll be meeting your daddy again a mite sooner than you figured.'

He spat on the carpet. 'You're scum, Wade Wallis, you know that. Worse scum than us. And that takes some doing. We asked round see, when you offered us your little job. We figured out what it is you got against Grice.'

Judd, who'd moved into the room, laughed. 'A frigging bag of beans. Takes a real man to hold a grudge 'bout something like that, and pay another man to fix it for him!'

'How'd you find out about that?'

Crouch shook his head. 'You drink too much, and talk too much, mister. A lot of whining talk, too. 'Bout how wicked the world's been to you. Kind o' feller who blames everyone 'cept himself!'

Wallis sat down again, and felt sick to the deepest part of his stomach. He'd been having a dream, and now the gilt had flaked off to show him the real nightmare underneath. 'What do you want me to do?'

Rosco listened impassively to what Broleen and Emmy had to say for themselves, just shaking his head now and again. When they'd finished the story, he leaned back in his chair, and mulled it over in a slow, thoughtful way.

At last he broke a hole in the silence. 'I never heard nothing like it. Trying to fire a whole town with the idea of a ghost coming back for vengeance.' He shook his head. 'But you sure have started a fire just as hot as the one burned that old cabin. Or the one that fried Jude Wallis last night.'

'I'd stake my life that wasn't Ethan Grice's doing,' Broleen burst out.

'It's his life I'm worried 'bout, not yours,' countered Rosco. 'But I'd say you were right. Ethan's no killer. But if he didn't do it ...' He raised a hand, seeing Emmy trying to get a word in. 'And don't start blaming Abel Cray again, you hear?'

Emmy pressed her hands together. 'I'm not going to do that sheriff, but just suppose....just suppose there is some kind of connection. Willy Candell and Jude Wallis were pretty close back then. Suppose Wallis was one of those tied up in the cabin fire.'

Rosco sighed. 'You keep coming back to that, Miss Scales. You don't even know for sure that Willy Candell had anything to do with it. It was a fire. Dried out wood burns real quick in times like these. Saw that last night.'

Broleen straightened up. 'You saying that my mother was a liar, Rosco?'

Rosco shook his head. 'No, I ain't saying she was a liar. But Willy Candell sure was. A boasting, cheating liar, 'specially when he was drunk. And by your ma's account, on that night he was roaring drunk.'

'She thought he was telling the truth.' There was

a dangerous edge in Broleen's voice. 'And I believe her.'

The lawman shrugged, 'Don't get us no further, though, does it? Candell shot himself. Jude Wallis got set afire. Two things don't slot together at all.'

Broleen walked over to the desk, and stared down at the sheriff. 'And how about Rufus Jepp?' he asked sharply. 'I just remembered how twitchy Wallis got when I told him Jepp'd been found with a slug in his head.'

'More like his skull than his head,' remarked Rosco. 'How do you mean, twitchy?'

'Sweating like a hog, and not just 'cause of the heat. He was scared, Rosco. Maybe scared for his life.'

Rosco let out a whistle. 'Hell, you two! You're straining at this harder than an ox at a loaded wagon. Jepp was robbed, that's all. Nothing to do with Jude Wallis.'

'But Rufus *was* around back in those days! Working as a cowpuncher. He only got religion later on.' Emmy worked furiously to think this one out. 'Suppose....'

'Here we go again,' muttered Rosco wearily.

'Suppose that me and Buzz really stirred something with our....crazy tale. If Candell was telling the truth, the fire at Polanski's cabin was no accident. There were other men involved in whatever happened. And now one of those men is trying to keep the rest from talking.'

He stared hard at her, and she saw that there was a glimmer of doubt in his eyes. 'So you saying we got a murderer running round Victory, then?'

Broleen dived in quick. 'You got to admit it sounds likely, Rosco.'

'No I don't!' snapped the lawman. 'It don't sound likely at all.' He faltered, though. 'Well, who in hell is it, then? You tell me that.'

Emmy folded her arms, and bristled with an air of righteous indignation. 'Just the kind of question me and Buzz have been asking. All right, we went about it the wrong way. But you'll have to help us now, won't you, sheriff?'

'Me help you?' Rosco blustered. 'Listen, I'm the lawman. It's you folk'll be helping me....if'n when I decide there's a spit of truth in any of this.' He turned to Broleen, clearly set on saying something else, when he was distracted by a shout outside.

'Broleen. Buzz Broleen. You in there?'

'Who in hell's that?' Rosco leapt from his chair, and shoved past the other, staring through the grimed window.

Wade Wallis was standing out in the middle of the street, watched from a safe distance by a curious, growing crowd. He yelled again, 'Broleen? I want words with you.'

Broleen joined Rosco at the window. 'That's Jude Wallis's son. I've seen him in the saloon. Never spoken to him, though. What in hell does he want with me?'

'Looks drunk to me,' commented Rosco. He inspected Broleen with a flicker of suspicion. 'You had any dealings with his pa?'

'No,' Broleen replied. 'Had a few words with him in the hotel, that's all. Anyhow, like you say Rosco, that one looks like he's been filling himself with liquor. No harm in going to see what he wants.'

Nervously, Emmy speculated, 'Maybe he thinks you had something to do with his father's death, Buzz.'

Broleen shrugged, and hitched up his gunbelt. 'He's not wearing a gun, so I figure he's not set on revenge.'

'More likely to want to shake your hand.' Rosco scratched his nose slowly. 'I tell you, though, I don't like it. Him just standing there like that. It don't make sense.'

'You coming, Broleen?' Wade Wallis yelled again. He was standing there stiff as a statue, but then just for an instant he glanced back. They'd hardly have noticed the movement if they weren't watching him as unblinking as hawks.

Rosco gave a low, hissing whistle. 'There's someone pulling his strings, Broleen. Someone with a gun aimed at his head.' He glanced back at Emmy. 'You just get outa here. Through the door and into the cells. If lead's gonna start flying around you'll be safer in there.'

'Now hold on....' the girl began.

'Just git your pretty ass where I say. Else I'll help you with my boot!'

She disappeared without further protests, and the sheriff looked at Broleen. 'I can't see no-one out there, but I know they're there.'

'Harry Crouch?' asked Broleen.

'I figure. 'Less you made any other enemies round here.'

Broleen shook his head, 'Not any I can think of.'

Edging to the window, Rosco peered out again. Then he let out a long breath, as he saw the sun glinting on something metallic up on the flat roof of the feed store. 'I see 'em! You go out there, Broleen, and you'd be a leaking sieve before you had time to say your prayers.'

Wallis called once more. 'Broleen!'

'So we just sit it out?'

'The hell we do,' grunted Rosco in answer to Broleen's queston. He started to move back towards the far wall where he had his gun rack. 'I can get a shot in at those boys, easy. They want games, they can have them....!'

Then out there on the street, with so many eyes watching him, Wade Wallis's paper-thin nerve tore right down the middle, and he decided to run towards the sheriff's office. Broleen had once seen someone outrun a stampeding bull, but he'd never seen anyone with speed enough to win the race with a bullet. A shriek of agony lacerated the air as the first slug struck Wallis in the back, driving him off balance. Somehow he stayed upright, almost rolling with its impact as a boxer would roll with a punch. He staggered forward a few steps, one hand reaching out hopelessly, and then two more bullets ripped into him and his legs began to fold under him. He took a final, straining step and pitched forward onto his face.

Broleen sensed what was going to happen next. 'Get down, Rosco. We're next!'

The grimy window melted into a spraying cascade of glass slivers, as bullets buzzed in like angry wasps. Broleen stayed flat on the floor, knowing that it would be futile, and more than likely fatal to try exchanging fire with those men on the roof.

The storm of lead was over in no more than a few seconds, but Broleen lay there a while longer, just in case they were waiting for him to peer out of the jagged remains of the window. 'I guess they've gone, Rosco.' He eased himself up to look out at the street. Already the scattered crowd was reforming, slowly converging on the sprawled figure of Wade Wallis. 'How come they used him as a decoy?' he muttered.

Then instead of any kind of answer to his question, from behind him he heard a low moan. He spun round and saw Rosco lying on his back, struggling to get up. Blood seethed and bubbled from a rip in his chest, and as their eyes met Broleen knew there was no need to hide what Rosco already knew. The sheriff would be dead in minutes, if not sooner. Snatching the lawman's old jacket off its hook, Broleen balled it up, easing it under the dying man's head.

Rosco's eyes were glazing. 'I can't swear you in, Broleen. But the star's yours now. If you don't take it, then....' His eyes flickered shut, then opened again, 'Then I swear to God there'll be a real ghost round here.'

'Just don't talk, Rosco.' Footsteps clicked down the passageway leading from the cells and Emmy rushed in. As soon as she took in the scene, she walked slower, and Broleen saw that she knew her nurse's training was going to be no use here.

She sank to her knees beside the stricken man, and gripped his hand. Rosco was finding it an almost impossible effort to talk now. 'You're on your own with this one. You got to figure what to do.'

Emmy kept her hold on the sheriff's hand, and he tried to smile. 'See what I said,' he mumbled, no louder than a sigh. 'Man'd be prepared to die to get this one holding his hand....'

They were his last words. Mechanically, Broleen unclipped the star from the dead man's vest. Pushing himself to his feet, he pinned it on his own shirt.

'What are you doing, Buzz?' Emmy asked in alarm.

'Keeping a promise,' he told her. 'Only way I can make up now. If I wasn't here in this town, Emmy, then likely that man there'd still be breathing.'

'You can't blame yourself!'

He looked wordlessly at the woman he loved, still crouching there holding a dead man's hand. 'It's all got to be finished, Emmy. One way or the other.'

With that, Buzz Broleen dragged the door open, and walked out into the eye-burning brightness of the street.

EIGHT

The crowd was bunching up round where Wade Wallis lay stretched on his face. They gazed at Broleen speculatively, and then a rumbling muttering started as they saw he was wearing the lawman's badge.

'Rosco's dead,' Broleen told them bluntly.

For a moment there was a stunned silence. Then someone yelled, 'It was that snake Harry Crouch. I see him up there on the roof of the feed store!'

Another man shouted his own confirmation. 'Him and his murdering pals. What in hell were they playing at?'

Ignoring the commotion round him, Broleen tried to think things through. He stared down at Wade Wallis's body. 'Anybody got any idea how come they chose him?'

A grizzled cowhand stepped closer to him. 'For a start, mister, we ain't got no idea how come you're wearing that badge.'

Broleen stiffened. 'You figuring on taking it off me? Fancy taking a run at being sheriff yourself?'

Nearby, an old man recalled, 'I seen Wade Wallis jawing with Crouch and his boys in George's a few times. Figured he was fixing them to do some kinda job for him.'

'That so?'

The oldster nodded. 'I heard some tale that Ethan Grice, or maybe it was his missus, bent Wade's nose outa shape over something a while back.'

'So that's it,' snapped Broleen. 'Listen I need a dozen men! A dozen men for a posse to ride out and catch these murdering bastards.'

The crowd fell silent, and began to melt back from him. Broleen searched for some expression in the faces round him, but nobody gave anything away. His own face hardened. 'They missed out on killing me, and got Jake Rosco instead. That's your sheriff they've murdered. Don't that mean nothing?'

The old man sniffed. 'You ain't never gonna catch them, mister.'

'Maybe I will,' said Broleen. 'Could be they're headed for Ethan Grice's homestead.'

The grey-bearded cowpuncher finished rolling a smoke. 'I guess we're all real sorry about Rosco. But word is that Grice murdered Jude Wallis last night. If that's how it is, then I guess he's only gonna get what's coming to him.'

There was a grumble of agreement from those round him. Broleen fired a look of contempt at them. 'Grice didn't kill anyone.'

'Who was it then? Abel Cray?' The man's mocking question was drowned in laughter. It was the laughter of relief. They didn't have to risk their own lives. Harry Crouch might be headed for the homestead out beyond the Hogtail for all the wrong reasons; but in the end he'd be doing the right thing. Then he'd ride on out of their lives.

Someone else's problem then, not theirs.

'It won't just be Grice gets it!' snarled Broleen desperately. 'There's his wife, and what's left of his family. That must mean something to you.' But he knew it didn't mean enough to them for them to take any action, and Jake Rosco's dying words echoed back at him: *You're on your own with this one.*

The cowboy was still watching him. 'It ain't a whole lot to do with you, neither, mister. And anyhow, I don't figure Harry Crouch'll be heading that way. I figure he'll just high-tail it outa the county, outa the state. Outa everyone's hair!'

After another chorus of agreement, the cowpoke smirked. 'Even if he does stop by the Grice place, he ain't gonna do nothing to Grice's kids. So just stop fretting, mister.'

Broleen reached forward and yanked the smoke from his mouth, dropping it to the dirt. 'Maybe you're right, maybe you're wrong. But Grice is an innocent man. If he gets himself killed, his kids'll be losing a father. I just don't believe I'm hearing you right, cowboy. What kinda man are you?'

'You can't talk to me like that!'

'You're damn right! I've done with talking.' Seconds later and the other man was sprawled back on the ground, holding his jaw. Just in case of more trouble, Broleen whipped out his six-gun and addressed the gaping bystanders. 'Now if you're not going to help, just git outa here. And someone go fetch the undertaker. He's got business enough, even if nobody else has.'

Holstering his Colt, he strode back to the office. Emmy had covered Rosco with a blanket from one of the cots in the cell. She'd clearly kept an ear on what was going on out there. 'Do you really think Crouch'll go near Ethan's Grice's place, Buzz? He doesn't know Rosco's dead. But he shot Wade Wallis in the back. For all he knows there's a whole posse riding out after him.'

Broleen stared helplessly at her. 'Maybe so. But he's a vicious bastard. So I got no choice but to ride after him. Out to the Grice place.'

She grabbed at his hand. 'You can't do that. Not alone. Suppose he is there, waiting for you?'

'Then that's how it is.'

Emmy caught her breath. 'And if he isn't there?'

'Then I keep looking. Rosco's dead because of me. I owe it to him to bring Crouch in, dead or alive.'

'Not by yourself,' she gabbled. 'What about us, Buzz? What about our future?'

'I never was one for making plans,' he muttered. 'Not till I met you, Emmy. Always figured that making plans was like trying to catch smoke in your fist. I must do this. No matter how long it takes. I owe it to Ethan and Sal, too.'

She kept hold of his hand. 'This is crazy, Buzz. You'll get killed. I'll never see you again. And what about....?' She broke off.

'What were you going to say?'

With a last shake of her head she let go of his hand. 'It doesn't matter. You go, if that's what you have to do!'

'I'll be back before you know it,' promised Broleen hoarsely. He dragged her to him, and kissed her. She tried to hold on to him again, but he thrust her away.

Turning to the door, he found his way blocked by one of the men from the bank head office. The new arrival stared dazedly at the shape under the blanket. 'Is he dead?'

'Why don't you ask him!' Broleen fired back brutally. 'Now, get out of my way, mister.'

The bank official had seen the star now. 'Listen, if you're the new sheriff, you ought to see this.' He was flapping a piece of paper in Broleen's face. 'We found it....'

Broleen edged him to one side. 'Show it to my deputy there,' he barked, and pointed at Emmy. 'She's better at reading than me, anyhow.'

Then he was gone. Emmy rushed to the door, and watched him running down towards the livery. Fisher Maclaine the undertaker was already getting Wade Wallis's body loaded onto his cart, he'd be here in a minute or two.

She blinked back a tear or two as Broleen disappeared inside the livery building, but she was as good as dry-eyed when she swung back to look at the nervous, baffled bank man. No sense in crying for Broleen until she had to. And it was best to keep her mind occupied. 'So what've you got there?' she asked.

The man gave a worried shake of his head. 'I never heard of a woman being a sheriff's deputy. And I'm not sure....'

She grabbed the paper out of his hand. It was covered with lines of small, crabbed writing. 'What is this?'

'We found it in an old ledger between two pages pasted together. It's an unpleasant kind of story. I'm not too sure you should read it, miss.'

'He was an unpleasant kind of man.'

'Yes, he was. We knew he was a crook, but we didn't know he was a killer too.'

Emmy was already reading the first line: *To whom it may concern. This is the true story about the burning of Professor Polanski's cabin ...*

Her hand shook. 'He wrote it all down?'

The man nodded. 'That's what he did. Kept a record of what happened in case the truth ever came out. Didn't want to be the only one who was blamed. There's a list of all those men involved, too. He wrote it down, sealed it away in one of his ledgers, and forgot it was there.'

Fisher Maclaine put his head through the door. 'I've come to collect the deceased.' He blinked as he saw Emmy, 'What're you doing here, Miss Scales?'

'That's a good question, Mr Maclaine,' she replied dully. 'Come on in. We'll get out of your way. But you treat him carefully. He was a good man.'

Maclaine eyed her thoughtfully, 'Every man's a good man when he's dead.'

Emmy stepped on outside, still holding the paper. The man from the bank darted after her. 'Your name's Scales?'

'Emmeline Scales, sure,' she confirmed absently. 'What's yours?'

By way of answer he snatched the sheet of paper out of her hand. 'I just don't figure you should read that, miss. I really don't.'

'Now just you hold on,' she exclaimed. 'You heard what Buzz said. He told you to show that paper to me!'

With a shake of his head, the man folded it, and thrust it into his pocket. 'It can wait till Mr Broleen gets back.'

Emmy caught her breath as he strode back

rapidly towards the bank. 'It might be waiting a good long time, then!' she called after him.

Normally she would have fought back against that kind of treatment. Being treated like some delicate flower which'd bruise at the first breath of wind always riled her. Especially now, since she'd seen so much of life and death at that hospital in the little Ohio town. For now, though, she didn't have the energy in her for an argument.

She watched sadly as Maclaine's men carried Jake Rosco out of the office, and laid him on the cart, next to the shrouded body of Wade Wallis. A little shiver went through her as she wondered who might be next to be carried to the funeral parlour on that cart.

The undertaker came alongside her. He might look like an oversized buzzard with his white face, and his shabby black coat, but for all his hand-rubbing humility he knew more about human nature than most people did. 'You should get home, miss. There's nothing you can do here.'

'Except wait,' she murmured.

Fisher Maclaine climbed onto the seat of the cart, and moved off with his silent cargo. Emmy looked away from him down the street. It was quiet now, few people moving round. Doubtless the men who'd watched all that excitement were now filling the saloons, lubricating their dusty throats and picking over what had happened. Broleen would be riding hard, it shouldn't take him more than half an hour to get to the Grices' place. At least, for that thirty minutes she'd know that he was still alive.

Then she saw a cloud of dust heralding the approach of a rider. He was coming at a spanking pace, and for a moment she clutched at a wafer-thin wish that it might be Broleen. That he'd decided the odds were too great and had turned back. A little smile twitched her lips, even as the hope crumbled. That wasn't his way. He'd worn a lawman's badge once before. The marshal had been murdered in that Kansas town and Broleen had taken on the gang responsible.

He'd been pretty much alone then, too, from the guarded, vague account he'd given her. It seemed he'd spent a lot of time alone one way or another in the years between leaving home, and coming back to Ohio to watch his mother die.

'And men who live alone, generally die alone,' she murmured under her breath, recalling something her father had once said. She could see the rider now as he rapidly approached. A huge man on a huge horse. It was Deal Tyler.

With a sudden flicker of faint hope, Emmy stepped down from the sidewalk and waved to him, and he brought his mount to a dust-stamping stop. He glared down at her from the saddle. 'I said all I wanted to say to you, missie. Now I need a drink, so....'

'Please,' she begged. 'Just listen to me, Mr Tyler. I know you don't have too much time for me.'

He laughed humourlessly. 'Wonder how you figured that?'

'But yesterday, you said you'd given up trying to drive the nesters out....'

'What of it?'

'It's Harry Crouch, Mr Tyler. He's killed Jake Rosco, and Wade Wallis. Buzz Broleen's gone after him. We figure he's maybe gone to the Grice place. He might murder the whole family....'

He hardly seemed to hear her. 'Your pa in town with you?'

'No. I've been staying with a friend. But Mr Tyler, listen, maybe you could ride after Buzz. He needs help!'

He wasn't listening to what she was saying. There was a strange light in his sombre eyes. He eased himself down from the saddle. 'Seems he don't care too much about you, your pa. Sends you off to Ohio to learn fancy manners. Lets you go riding off wherever, whenever, you choose.'

His lips curled, and there was a note as bitter as the taste of stewed coffee in his voice. 'Used to work for me, you know, your pa. 'Fore he set up by himself.'

'I know that.' She tried once more. 'Please Mr Tyler! If you rode out now, you could catch up with him.' But she realised it was useless. Whatever he had on his mind was blocking out everything else.

'Had a lotta time for Benton Scales,' he mused. 'Married a real pretty gal. Your ma, that was. Had a real pretty daughter. How old was you when I lost my Charlotte?'

Emmy shrugged uneasily. 'Five years old maybe.'

Tyler gave a long, rasping sigh. 'I guess you were. Now you'd be about the same age she was when Abel Cray took her from me. Wonder how your pa'd feel if he had to look at you all black and burned and shredded half to ash by flames.'

He reached out a big hand to her, and touched her cheek. All at once, without knowing why, Emmy wanted to run. 'There was a breeze a-blowing up when they showed me to her.' His lips contorted in a snarl of pain. 'A breeze blowing and taking my Charlotte with it, like she was pepper spilled on a table.'

Now his hand moved, and clamped onto her shoulder, his nails biting into her under the thin cotton. 'Mr Tyler you're hurting me!' she protested.

'Not near so much as I was hurting that day!' He released her and she rubbed at her shoulder. 'You get inside that office, Emmy. I got other things to say to you.'

'Listen,' she cried desperately. 'I was trying to explain about Buzz. He needs your help. You can tell me all this later.'

She looked round wildly, but Victory looked as deserted as a ghost town in the shimmering heat. Tyler slung his horse's reins over the hitch pole, and tied them with the deftness of long years practice. 'I said, get inside.'

His boots clumped noisily up the steps after her, accompanied by the jangle of his spurs. She moved beyond Rosco's desk, and pressed herself against the wall. He crunched over the broken glass and rested his hands on the desk, leaning forward as he stared at her, pushing down hard with splayed fingers.

Emmy's teacher at college had always laughed away the idea that instinct could give a person insight. Facts, evidence, they were the only things that mattered in getting at the truth. But looking at the big rancher now, standing like that, his hand pressing down on the edge of the desk, Emmy's instinct jabbed her sharper than a knife. She moistened her lips with her tongue. 'You killed Willy Candell, Mr Tyler, didn't you? You were there in his office....'

There was not the slightest flicker of reaction on his face.

Shakily, she went on, 'Buzz got at the truth without knowing it, didn't he? That smudging he saw, in Candell's blood. It really was the mark of a man's fingers. *Your* fingers!'

Tyler straightened up sharply. 'Bright as a button, ain't you? Jus' like my poor sweet Charlotte. And likely just as foolish, getting caught up with a feller who ain't worthy of you.'

'But how did you do it? And why?'

'As to how,' he grunted. 'I pulled a trigger and blasted out his wicked brains.'

'The door was locked!'

The rancher nodded. 'Sure it was. But he had two door-keys on his chain. Guess he'd been meaning to give one to his cashier and never gotten round to it. So I was able to get outa there and leave the door locked. As to why I killed him. I guess you know that, Emmy, being so blasted bright and all.'

'He was one of those responsible for your daughter's death?'

Tyler's eyes blazed. 'Responsible? Sure. One of a whole bunch of murdering scum!'

'But how did you find that out?' she demanded.

He shrugged. 'Rufus Jepp told me. Come to see me that same day. What with this drought and all, reminding him of that time, and the anniversary coming round again, he wanted to clear his conscience 'fore he came into town to hand himself into the sheriff.'

He spat on the floor. 'Said how he'd taken to religion because of what he and the rest'd done that day. But it never give him no peace.' Tyler paused. 'Well, I helped him out there. Got all the peace he needs now.'

Emmy shivered. 'Mr Rosco and I found what was left of him, out by that dried up waterhole near your place. He'd been shot.'

With a bleak smile, Tyler growled, 'I knew nobody'd get hung for a crime sixteen years old. Not Jepp, nor those he said was there with him. So I done the law's job for it. Rode out with him to that waterhole. He knew what was in my mind, I figure. One shot. Quicker'n he deserved. Left him for the wolves and the buzzards. Still got his mule at my place.'

'And he told you who else was involved?'

'Going on for a dozen, there was,' he said. 'Jepp, Candell ... feller name of Sam Bute. He's been dead ten years. Marty Steele. He was a gambling man. Never did know what happened to him. Couple other fellers long gone outa these parts.'

'Jude Wallis?' Emmy hazarded.

Tyler nodded briskly. 'Him too. And you know what I done to him. Just wished I could of stuck around to see him fry to a crisp.' His face hardened to an iron mask, 'He was the one come to tell me that they'd pulled Charlotte outa that cabin. Hell, I cried in his arms when I seen her. I knew he'd need something special to finish him.'

Emmy was beyond fear now. She just felt numb, confused about his purpose in telling her all this. Maybe she'd just reminded him of his daughter. Maybe it was that, maybe it was something else.

He talked on, the words spilling out in a torrent. 'I guess Willie Candell was behind most of it. Abel Cray scared the shit outa him. And maybe he was just aiming to scare them, talking those fellers into going off with him that night to Polanski's cabin.'

Emmy's heart pounded as Tyler told her how the men, fresh from a night's drinking surrounded the cabin out on Jawbone Flat. 'Made a lotta noise, firing in the air. Hell, I got my own men to do that kinda thing. Just spook the nesters off of the land, that's all. Live men generally shift themselves quicker than dead ones.'

He stopped for a moment, staring at something she couldn't see. Then his voice hoarse with emotion, he carried on, 'There was some cans of kerosene stacked outside. Someone fired a shot into them. Caught fire, and the flames spread to the cabin real quick like it would with everything so dry....'

'And they stood by and let them burn?'

Tyler shook his head. 'Did more'n that. Every time someone tried to get outa there, they blasted a few shots to send 'em back. Jepp figures that Polanski got hit, but nobody'll ever know that for sure. Flames and smoke gotta hold, and pretty soon it was all over.'

'Did they know Charlotte was in there?'

'I guess one woman screaming as she blazes sounds much the same as another,' he replied, suddenly calm, 'Polanski's wife was in there, and his daughter too. Don't matter whether they know or not. Fact is, she was in there, and she died with the rest of 'em.'

His shoulders sagged for a moment, then he pulled himself up straight, and his eyes blazed with his own inner fire. 'Well, I've almost done now, Emmy. I thought revenge'd be sweet, but it ain't at all. But it's gotta be done.'

'Almost done?' she repeated.

'Sure,' he replied. 'Just one left now. Just one.'

There were others heading for the Grice homestead, as Broleen cut down through the parched trees fringing the stony edges of the Hogtail. Half a mile off maybe. Half a dozen men coming as fast as their lumbering mules would bring them. Other homesteaders, who'd maybe heard something happening here, and came as quick as they could. Like him, they were too late. Everywhere was silent here, except for the subdued clucking of a few thin chickens scratching in the dusty yard.

Broleen knew, with a sickening certainty, that Crouch had completed the job which Wade Wallis had paid him to do, and gone on his wicked way. His horse had its head down; there was no hurrying it now, it took each step reluctantly, and Broleen knew that the animal's keen nostrils had picked up the smell of death.

A few yards from the fence, Broleen swung down, and finished the journey on foot, passing the new-made mound with its rough wooden cross where the family's only son was buried. He saw Ethan Grice first, huddled near the cabin door, brought down by a single shot in the back. Maybe he'd seen them coming, been running to warn his family; knowing it was hopeless.

The door gaped, and Broleen stepped inside. It was as bad as he'd imagined it would be. There was nothing he could do, except try to give back those violated bodies some kind of human dignity. When he came out a minute or two later, his face was stiff as cold steel, and he walked like a man in a trance. The dust cloud raised by the approaching nesters was nearer now, and he was glad those men wouldn't have to see things quite as bad as he'd seen them.

There was no sign of Sal Grice or Josie, the little girl, though, not in there. He closed his eyes for a moment, and a jagged spear of rage and sorrow sliced into his heart. As he moved away from the cabin, out of the corner of the eye he saw movement over by the makeshift old barn. His sidearm was already in his hand as he spun round.

'Mister, mommy's hurt real bad.'

The Grices' youngest daughter stood looking pleadingly at him. Josie's face was tearstained, and there were blotchy smudges of blood all over her cotton dress.

He found Sal Grice just inside the barn, slumped against a wall. There was a bloody rent in the front of her apron, and her head lolled forward. The small girl was behind him as he crouched by her mother's side. The woman was still breathing. 'Sal, can you hear me?'

The dying woman raised her head, and opened her eyes. Her lips were flecked with blood and she spoke haltingly. 'Mr Broleen. I knew you'd come.'

'Too late, though, Sal, too late.' He choked back a sob, as the child came round him, and held onto her mother's hand.

'They never got Josie,' she mumbled. 'You'll see to her. I know you will.'

'Sure I will. And I'll get Crouch for this.'

She stared unblinking at him. 'Ethan, and the twins....'

He couldn't lie to her, and she didn't want him to. 'They're dead, Sal.'

She was forcing every word out now, and it reminded him of the way his mother had spoken at the end. 'But they died quick. All of 'em. Didn't they, Mr Broleen?'

This time she was begging him to lie to her. Sal knew what men crazed with drink, and blood-lust were capable of doing. She knew how pretty her daughters were. She know how it might have been for Mary and Ellen, but she prayed it hadn't been like that. 'Sure,' he said. 'Sure Sal. They all died real quick. Didn't suffer, none.'

'You're a good man, Broleen,' she said huskily. 'Well, they ain't suffering now, anyhow.' She turned her eyes from him. 'Josie, my sweet little Josie. You gotta be a good girl. You'll grow up a fine woman, I know.'

Broleen wiped his eyes as he stood up. Sal's eyes were shut now, and they'd never open again. 'You come with me, Josie now. Your ma's at peace now.'

Obediently the child took his hand, and he led her back into the blazing sunlight. The yard was no longer deserted. They stood there watching him and the girl, five or six men bunched close by, all wearing heavy boots, bib overalls and linsey shirts. A couple were bearded; most packed some variety of rifle. Beyond the fence, their mules joined his horse in nuzzling at such sparse tufts of grass as they could find.

'Uncle Zeke!' Josie Grice let go of Broleen's hand and ran to one of the bearded men, who swung her up in his arms, comforting the sobs which erupted from her.

One of the nesters stepped a pace or two towards Broleen. He'd been among those outside the gunsmith's when Matt Grice had been killed.

'They made you sheriff, then?'

'Jake Rosco's dead,' he told them dully. 'Killed by Harry Crouch and his boys. I rode here after them. I was too late.'

'We was all too frigging late, mister,' said another of the nesters bitterly. 'We was meeting with Ethan today, to decide how to fight the ranchers. Now they done killed him. You see what they done to those sweet girls?'

'Sure, I've seen it. But Crouch wasn't working for Tyler, or any other rancher. He was being paid by Wade Wallis. That one had some kinda grudge against the Grices. Now he's dead, too.'

'So you say!'

'It's true, man, I tell you,' Broleen insisted. 'Nobody wants a range war.'

'Maybe they don't!' barked another of the steaders. 'But I figure that's what they got. You knew Crouch was headed this way?'

'I figured he might come.'

The bearded man holding the child spoke. 'How come nobody else rode with you?'

"Cause they wouldn't give a toe-nail clipping for any of us!' snarled the nester nearest to Broleen. 'That's why. Well some fine folks died here today, and someone's gonna pay for that!'

'Crouch'll pay, and his pals!' Broleen fired back. 'Even if I have to ride for the rest of my life to catch up with them.'

'You do what you have to, mister,' muttered the nester. 'And we'll do what we have to. And right now that means giving these folks a decent burying.'

'Sure, that's the first thing to do.'

Even as he spoke, though, they all heard a

rattle of gunfire from somewhere high up on the Hogtail Ridge. Broleen tensed, listening. The echo of the shots drifted off into the sky, and he moved, taking the ground between him and the fence in a few loping strides. Clearing the fence, he whistled his horse over.

He looked back at the nesters, as he swung into the saddle. 'Maybe Crouch and his gang aren't so far away.'

'You don't know that shooting's got anything to do with them!' declared the man holding Josie Grice.

'No, I don't. But I aim to go and find out if it does!'

NINE

Broleen didn't know or care whether the nesters had taken it into their heads to follow him as he turned his mount up through the ragged trees, and onto the steepening, stony slopes of the Hogtail. He traced the course of that climbing track hacked out long ago by those miners bent on seeking out that legendary silver seam which he recalled his father telling him about. There'd been no fortune of any kind for most of the silver prospectors. Such ore deposits as had been found quickly gave out, leaving a few men richer and a goodly number a whole lot deader, since the Sioux in those days had seen their pack mules, tools and supplies as a tempting target.

All the time Broleen kept listening for a repeat performance of that scattering of gunfire, hoping he was pointed in the right direction. His nose told him that Crouch and his henchmen were round here somewhere; it was an exchange of fire he'd heard, he was sure of that. Which could just mean that someone else, maybe another homesteader, had taken it into their heads to go after that murdering gang.

He sensed that his horse was getting nervy now, spooked by the surrounding rocks, and finding the steeply rising track tough going. Broleen dismounted, leading the animal for a couple of hundred more yards, before coming on a small plateau curving away from the track.

'You stay here, feller.' He slapped the beast's flank, 'And don't go wandering off over the edge.' The animal's ears pricked, and he unhooked his Winchester from behind the saddle. 'I'll be back 'fore you know I've gone.'

A wry grin played on his lips as he headed swiftly on up the old trail. Crazy thing to do, saying goodbye to your horse like it was your wife or something. The grin faded though, and a guilty twinge went through him, as he recalled his curtly hurried parting with Emmy. Hell, he'd been more polite to his horse than he had to her. His mother always used to say that you should always part with folks on friendly terms, just in case something bad happened to them before you met again.

'If that happens, son, you'll always regret it. You mark my words.'

'I'm going to see Emmy again!' he mumbled. 'And I'll make it up to her soon as I get back.'

Thinking about her now, he realised he'd never again feel the exhilaration which danger had once brought him. In the past, he'd squared up to men twice his size, risked everything as easily as he might wait for a coin to fall the right way up. Because it hadn't mattered then which way the coin fell. Now it did matter; he wanted to see Emmy again, hold her close, and smell the sweetness of her, and he just hoped to hell that the man in the sky was taking account of that wish right now.

Suddenly gloomy, he carried on along the zig-zagging trail, skidding now and then on the loose drifts of dried out shale which crunched dustily and noisily under the soles of his boots. It was hard going in this heat, and a couple of times he raised a shower of sweat when he had to clamber over an old rockfall. The only sound was the noise of his feet grinding into the crackling shale. The track cut along just beneath the jagged backbone of the ridge, broken in places, giving him a view across the other side towards the Blue Valley, and the Hanging B where Emmy had been born and brought up.

Then for a moment he thought the track had come to an end at a sheer wall of rock, but then saw there was a wide fissure in the ridge into which the trail turned itself. He edged into that natural gateway blinking against the blinding sunlight. They always said you heard the sound of the shot that killed you just as the bullet hit. He heard the sound of this particular shot the same instant that a slug slapped viciously against a rock close to his head, and ricocheted away from him.

A splinter of flying rock tore a gouge in his cheek but he was already on his knees as the next bullet buzzed above him.

'You was damn lucky there, mister!'

The man was watching him from a rocky scoop just below the gap in the ridge. Broleen scrambled down to where he was sitting, leaning back, his rifle laid across his knees. To their left, the miners' trail curved away, disappearing out of sight. Broleen fingered the gash on his cheek.

The other man surveyed him with rough

sympathy. He was stockily-built, big shouldered. His thinning hair had been black once, now it was liberally speckled with grey. 'Hell, it ain't no more'n a scratch. You ain't gonna bleed to death.' A touch shakily, Broleen slumped down next to the stranger, who extended a hand. 'Benton Scales.'

Broleen hesitated before shaking hands. 'Is that so? Name's Broleen.' He searched the other man's face, trying in vain to find some likeness there to the woman he loved. But then Emmy always said she took her looks from her mother, and her stubbornness from her father. 'I've heard of you Mr Scales. What in hell you doing here, and...?'

'I've heard of you too, Broleen,' cut in the rancher. 'How you already had dealings with those fellers down below us.' Like the nesters down at the homestead, he slapped a curious look on to the star ornamenting Broleen's shirt.

'Jake Rosco's dead!' snapped Broleen. 'Killed by those fellers down there.'

'And you've taken over?'

'Looks like it. They all down there? Crouch and his boys?'

'Sure are,' Scales confirmed. 'The track leads on down to some old mine workings. They're holed up in what's left of the cabin.' He twisted round. 'Wouldn't recommend sticking your noddle over the rocks, but if you press your eye 'gainst that hole there ...' He indicated with a thick, tobacco-yellowed finger.

Broleen peered through the gap in the rocks; too narrow to get a shot through, but he could see down to the old cabin clear enough. The men's horses were tied nearby, and he spotted movement behind the crumbling cabin walls. He rested his back against the rock again. 'Maybe we can't get a shot at them without getting our own heads blown off, but I don't figure they can go anywhere.'

'Kinda stalemate, sure.'

Rolling himself a smoke, Broleen asked cautiously, 'You know what they've done, mister? They've near on wiped out Ethan Grice and his family.'

'I figured it might be that way,' muttered Scales. 'I was out on the far side of the Flat this morning. Tracking this pesky old wolf that's been taking out some of my stock. Heard shooting and came riding. Saw Crouch and his boys just heading out from the homestead.'

'They didn't see you?'

Scales shook his head. Reaching out, he took the smoke off Broleen, taking a couple of deep draws before handing it back. 'Figured I had two choices. Go see if I could help the 'steaders out, or follow Crouch.'

'I guess you made the right choice,' muttered Broleen. 'Wasn't nothing you could do there.'

'All dead?'

'The young one, she's alive. Unharmed.' Broleen paused, reflecting that Josie's wounds might not show, but there'd be part of her that would always be hurting. 'So you followed them?'

'I kept my distance,' returned Scales. 'Lost sight of them for couple of minutes, but three horses moving on this loose rock make one hell of a ruckus. I figured they was coming to these old workings, so I scrambled up here, got myself settled. Loosed off a few shots when I heard them arriving. They threw a few back at me. Now all we gotta do is wait.'

'There'll be others here soon enough,' said Broleen. 'It's been one hell of a morning. Rosco dead, and Jude Wallis and his boy.'

He heard the man next to him haul in a long breath. 'Crouch killed Jude and Wade Wallis?'

'Well he sure gunned down Wade,' replied Broleen. 'But Jade burned to death. In fact Victory's having more buryings than's decent, I'd say. Willy Candell, Rufus Jepp....'

'That old preacher's dead, too?'

Broleen glanced at him. 'I guess you won't have heard that neither. He was found out over near Deal Tyler's place yesterday. What was left of him.'

Scales ran a finger along the muzzle of his rifle. 'He was a sieve-headed old varmint. But there wasn't no real harm in him. Emmy ... that's my girl, she'll be real sorry to hear 'bout old Rufus.'

The only response Broleen made to that was a swift nod. This wasn't the time to tell the rancher that Emmy had been with the sheriff when he'd come upon the preacher's remains. And he surely wasn't going to tell Scales that he'd spent last night cuddled up in bed next to his daughter. For a moment or two the other seemed lost in drifting, sombre reflection about something, then he snapped out of it. 'Just what did Crouch have against Ethan Grice?'

'I don't rightly know that,' confessed Broleen. 'Seems that Wade Wallis was paying him to cause that family misery.'

'Some old grudge, maybe, that'd figure. And it'd be Wade's way.'

'Well, whatever,' Broleen said. 'Now all the nesters've got it into their heads that the ranchers are set on pushing them out.'

Scales wiped his brow. 'That was how it was once. Not now. Daresay there's room enough for us all. Couple of good rainy seasons and this'll all blow over.'

'Providing the lid doesn't blow off in the meantime.' Peering through that crack in the rocks again, Broleen's gaze flickered from the restlessly moving horses, to the tumbledown cabin. He watched for a good long while. He spotted Harry Crouch and then caught a glimpse of the man called Mickey, whose teeth he'd smashed out the other day.

As he continued to scan the cabin, Scales tapped him on the arm. 'You gone to sleep there, mister?'

Broleen rolled back round. 'I get a twitchy feeling about this, Mr Scales. Crouch is crazier than a drunk Comanche, but he's no fool. Yet he's just setting there, knowing he'll be surrounded 'fore long. No way out without getting gunned down.'

The rancher gave a puzzled shrug. 'He's got no choice. He'll make some kinda fight of it, I guess when it comes.'

'Maybe,' agreed Broleen doubtfully. 'And maybe I'll just check something out!'

'What you doing, you crazy buzzard!' yelled Scales, as Broleen snatched up his Winchester, and heaved himself above the protecting parapet of rock. He just had time to loose of a couple of wild shots, and then a responding volley of lead fanned his face, and ripped the shoulder of his shirt, singeing the hairs on the side of his neck.

Fastening a hefty hand round Broleen's ankle,

Scales yanked him back down to safety. He glowered hotly. 'You want to get your head blown off?'

Broleen shook himself. 'Got what I wanted. Saw the muzzle flashes. Just two. Mr Scales. There's just two guns down there. Three horses, but just two men. You said you lost sight of them for a while. Maybe they'd spotted you. Could be that Judd, the other one cut away ...'

'Then where is he?' interrupted Scales irritably. 'Listen, maybe only two of 'em are firing. Could be they're short on ammunition.'

'And could be they ain't!' From up above them there was the click of a firing hammer, and Broleen twisted round and stared up into the grinning face of Crouch's other henchman. 'Don't neither of you make a move.'

Then Judd raised his voice, 'I got 'em, Harry. Benton Scales and Sheriff Broleen!' His words echoed back from the surrounding rocks of the Hogtail. He laughed. 'Now you let those weapons drop, and go down and ... pay your respects to Mr Crouch. Real careful, else you're dead meat!'

The two prisoners slithered down the last few yards of track, with Judd following at a cautious distance. Emerging from the cabin, Crouch gave a whoop of malevolent glee. 'I knowed you'd be after me, Broleen. Should of stayed back in Victory. How come you wearing that fancy badge?'

'You got Rosco's blood on your hands, as well as all the rest!'

'Well, I ain't crying 'bout that,' scoffed Crouch. 'Blood washes off easy enough.'

'Don't look like your pal there does much washing!'

Micky's ugly face contorted with seething anger. 'Let me at him, Harry. I'll smash his teeth down his throat for him.'

'He's gonna be losing a bit more'n his teeth, boy,' snapped Crouch, whose gaze slewed to the man standing next to Broleen. 'We ain't got nothing 'gainst you, Scales. You just git outa here. Go for help maybe, but it won't do no good. This one....' The heavy six-gun wheeled meaningfully in Broleen's direction, 'Well, he'll be dead when you get back. And we'll be gone too.'

Broleen's eyes roved restlessly round the abandoned mine site, trying to find anything which might help him get out of this. He couldn't see much that would work that trick for him. There were a few discarded, rusting tools piled carelessly by the spoil heap. Near the shaft which had been cut horizontally into the rock face beyond the rotting cabin, he saw the remains of a makeshift old cart.

He stared into Crouch's bruise-blotched face. 'There's half a dozen nesters down at the Grice place, blood-mad at what you did. Could be they'll be waiting for you.'

Behind him, Judd cackled, 'Nah, they ain't. Still busying digging holes for their pals. Nobody cares 'bout you, Broleen.'

Crouch was growing impatient. 'Listen, Scales, I told you to get outa here.'

Broleen glanced regretfully at the rancher, 'Do like he says, Mr Scales. No sense in us both getting killed. One of us has got to stay alive for Emmy. When you see her, give her my love, will you?'

Scales stared disbelievingly, 'Give her your *what*?'

'Just tell her ... say I'm sorry. I guess that's all I can say when it comes to it.'

'You never said you knew my girl, Broleen! Something going on between you two?' Almost forgetting where he was, his eyes glittered with a father's suspicion. 'Just what is Emmy to you?'

At the back of them, Judd belched out another of his cackling laughs. 'Hell, Broleen, be worth keeping you alive so you could tell us just what you have been doing with that gal. I'll bet she's hot as chilli in the sheets, ain't she? And the jugs she's got on her....'

The moment Judd spoke those words, it flashed through Broleen's mind that the man might have the whole of eternity to regret what he'd said. Scales could likely be as foul-mouthed and rough talking as any man, but hearing his beloved daughter spoken of like that sent an unthinking, searing rage through him. There was a kind of blur as he swung round, so fast that none of the gang had any time to respond.

The next instant he hurled himself into Judd, lifting the gunman off his feet. With a rock-shaking, blistering roar, he sent him flying towards Crouch and Micky. As Judd cannoned into them, the three men crashed together to the ground in a dust-raising, cursing tangle. It gave Broleen the chance to dive for the revolver which had dropped from Judd's fist.

Mickey was the first to find his feet, goggling toothlessly and a touch dazed. His senses came back quickly enough, and he was still keeping hold of his gun, but before his finger could circle the trigger, Broleen sent two rapid shots stabbing his way. The first caught him low in the belly and, as the hole in his gut seethed scarlet and he buckled, the second slug blew the top of his head off. He was already dead when his flailing body jack-knifed into Judd, spinning the other man off balance, diverting the shot meant for Broleen into empty air.

Broleen triggered again as Judd began to twist back, and the slug burned into the man's shoulder, smashing the collar bone, and forcing a shriek of agony from between his lips. He slammed to the rocky ground, and lay writhing, and howling as if a red hot poker was being jammed into his bowels.

Amidst it all, Harry Crouch just sat there with an unconcerned grin, leaning back, with his hands planted on the ground. His own weapon lay a couple of yards out of his immediate reach. Shouting above the noise Judd was making he suggested, 'Finish him, Broleen. He ain't no good to nobody.'

'Then he's not worth wasting a slug on.' Broleen scowled with contempt. 'Same goes for you. I want to see you kicking at the end of a rope, Crouch. Never mind all the killing, you've near on started a war in Brady County.'

Crouch scratched his ear. 'The big men've gone soft round here.' He gave Benton Scales a mocking grin. 'Time was when nester scum'd be driven off a man's land as soon as look at 'em. You and Deal Tyler and the rest, you done gone flabbier than wet fish.'

'Just get on your feet!' Broleen barked.

'I figure I'll stay here a while longer,' drawled Crouch languidly. 'Hell, Judd will you quit that noise!'

For a split second Broleen's attention switched to that wounded man squirming and squealing next to the lifeless body of Micky. It was a natural human reaction, and Crouch had been banking on it. Flinging himself sideways, he got a hand to his revolver.

Broleen's instinct was already taking command of his body, and his head, and his gun-hand were both coming back round. Trouble was, Benton Scales was in his way. Two shots rang out. The first came from Harry Crouch's gun, and Scales took the blast in his chest; the second shot was Broleen's, and it drilled a bloodily blossoming hole straight into the hoodlum's evil brain.

Suddenly sickened by it all, Broleen's hand went limp and he let his gun fall. If Brady County was a river it'd be running red right now. Two men dead here, the best part of a decent family slaughtered; Rosco, Jude Wallis and his son.... Now there was Emmy's father, half lying, half sitting with a hand pressed futilely against his body, and blood pulsing through his fingers.

They said the west was growing up, but it didn't seem to be that way, not right now. He crouched beside Scales, whose face was grey with pain. 'Finish the other one,' he gasped. 'Save the county the cost of a rope. Man talks like that about my Emmy don't deserve to live....'

'I guess he don't,' muttered Broleen. 'But I need him alive, Mr Scales. Nesters'll need proof that Crouch wasn't being paid by Tyler, or you, or anyone else.'

Scales winced as a surge of pain throbbed through him. 'Guess you're right, Broleen. You ... got something going with my Emmy?'

'Just try not to talk,' urged Broleen. 'Let me take a look at the wound.'

'What for? I'm a dead man.' He coughed, 'You'll do the right thing by Emmy? She's a fine gal. Worth ten of most.'

'Twenty, I'd say.' Broleen nodded, 'I aim to marry her, Mr Scales. If you got no objection.'

'Hell, I can't stop you.' He was fading fast now, but trying to stay alive just a little longer. 'You just be good to her, you hear? Now, I got something else I need to say.'

'Sure,' said Broleen gently. 'I'm listening.'

'I done a lot of wrong things in my life, Broleen. But one was a whole lot worse'n any other. Hell, I was drunk. Times was bad for me. Maybe I didn't even know what I was doing....'

His eyes closed, and for a moment, Broleen thought he was gone, but something was forcing Scales to keep himself alive a little longer, and he opened his eyes again, and squeezed a few more words out of himself. 'I guess I always knowed I'd own up in the end. But it was all so damn long ago....'

'Mr Tyler! Will you let me out of here?' Emmy gripped the bars of the lock-up door, rattling them impotently, then gave up and sat down again on the edge of the narrow cot. She was miserably hot, achingly hungry and thirsty. There was just one small window high up in the slope of the roof, and from the angle of the sun cutting through the grime on the glass she calculated she'd been locked in here for over two hours.

He hadn't been in to look at her since he'd pushed her down the passage and into the cell, and for all she knew he was no longer in the outer office. What Deal Tyler was playing at, she had no real idea. If he wanted to keep her from spreading the news about his murderous trail of revenge for his lost daughter, then shutting her in here was scarcely the way to do it. Someone would find her eventually. She hoped to God it would be Buzz.

If only he hadn't ridden out like that. She should have finished telling him that one piece of news which might have made him stay. Under her breath she muttered, 'You're going to be a daddy, Buzz, and you might die without knowing it.'

Standing up again, she flapped her skirt round her legs, trying to raise some air, but it didn't do much good. She was soaked through with sweat, and her sodden clothes were clinging to her more closely than was decent. She was just glad there wasn't a glass in here for her to see just how bad she was looking.

'Alaska,' she remembered. 'That's where I want to be right now. Cold, shimmering ice and snow....'

The door at the end of the short passage swung open with a complaining creak, and Deal Tyler stamped down, holding the key to the lock-up in his fist. There was a kind of staring quality to his eyes, and a taut expression on his heavy-jowled face.

He yanked the door open, and she slid out. 'You've decided to let me go then?'

He didn't say anything, but as she tried to walk towards that open door, his hand closed on her arm. 'You're going nowhere, Emmeline,' he growled tonelessly. 'I just had to think what I was doing.'

She stumbled a little as he forced her along the

corridor, and back into the main office, the floor still scattered with glass. Emmy stopped just inside the door. 'Mr Tyler, I'll cut my feet to ribbons walking in there. I've taken my boots off!'

'It don't matter!' He didn't force her any further, though, and walked on past her, his booted feet crunching on the smashed remains of the window pane. Turning slowly, he fixed her with a long stare, and that baffled resentment she'd felt while sitting in the cell suddenly shifted sideways and became biting fear.

'I figured your daddy'd come looking for you.'

'Why should he do that? He doesn't know I'm here.'

Tyler's eyes narrowed, 'Should still come looking. Well, since he ain't, then he needs teaching.'

Stretching a hand over to Rosco's desk, he picked up his heavy .44 Navy Colt which was lying there. 'Bible says the sins of the fathers'll be visited on their children, don't it?'

Emmy shivered. She'd known Deal Tyler most of her life. Not well, maybe, but this man with his brooding, contorted face was a complete stranger. 'Sins? I don't know what you mean.'

'Said there was one left, didn't I? Jus' one. Candell's gone, Rufus Jepp, Jude Wallis. Only one left I can deal with now.'

Maybe she'd already started to reach out for the truth, sitting there alone in the cell, but her heart wouldn't accept what her brain was trying to tell her. The man from the bank had given her that sheet of paper written long ago by Willy Candell, and then seized it off her. Snatched it away when he found out her name was Scales. There might be lots of reasons for him acting that way, but the one that made most sense, was because Benton Scales was one of the names on Candell's lists of his accomplices.

She stared into Tyler's expressionless face. 'You think that my father....' She couldn't bring herself to finish the sentence.'

'Ain't a matter of thinking it. He was one of 'em. I been waiting for him here. Waiting for him to come to you, like I'd of come to my girl.' The man's voice was thick with emotion, 'But maybe it's only justice that he should lose a daughter too. Being as he took mine from me.'

A hand went to her mouth. 'Mr Tyler, I can't believe that my father would have....'

'Sure you do,' he rasped. 'I see it in those pretty eyes of yours. Rufus Jepp told me. Benton Scales was there, with the rest. Whooping, hollering, as the cabin burned and those folks died. Now he's going to feel just how I felt then, and how I've felt ever since!'

Emmy couldn't move, her muscles seemed locked as Tyler raised the gun, and she saw his finger starting to curl round the trigger. Then, just as she was expecting to hear the shot, and find herself plunged into oblivion, the rancher staggered back, and the weapon flew from his hand. His head was straining back, and he seemed to be struggling.

'Get outa here!'

With the words roaring in her ears, Emmy forgot that her feet were bare, and ran wildly across the scatter of glass. Reaching the door, she threw herself out into the bright sunlight, and tripped onto her knees. She let out a gulping sob of relief, and then looked up, and gave a cry of astonishment. Somehow she'd expected the street to be deserted, but everyone in Victory seemed to be waiting out here. Someone helped her up, and remembering the broken glass, she looked down and saw there wasn't a mark on her feet, not even a scratch.

She looked at the man who'd helped her up; a grizzle-bearded cowpuncher. 'What's going on?'

'We figured you'd know that, ma'am,' he said. 'We knew you was in there with Mr Tyler, but he told everyone to stay away from the sheriff's office. Said he'd shoot the first feller came within twenty yards.'

Behind him, someone intoned piously, 'Didn't know what to do for the best, miss.'

'So you just stood here watching?' she asked coldly. Then with an offended toss of her head, she turned to look back at the sheriff's office. There seemed to be no logical explanation of what had happened in there. It had almost looked as if someone had yanked Tyler's hand back, forcing him to drop the gun before he could fire, and then grabbed him round the neck, holding him tight, allowing Emmy to make a run for it. That couldn't be; there'd been nobody else in the office. So it must have been Tyler who'd yelled at her to get out. Yet, she shook her head in confusion, it hadn't sounded like Tyler's voice.

'What's Tyler doing now?' she heard someone ask.

'I don't know,' she murmured, but as she spoke the rancher came out of the door. He stood there a moment, like a man in a dream, and then slowly, he staggered towards the silent, waiting crowd.

The cowboy tried to hold her back, but Emmy ran towards Deal Tyler, blocking his path. He gave her a long, sorrowing look, and there was shame in his eyes. 'Wasn't your doing, Emmy,' he muttered tonelessly, 'Killing you would have been a wicked thing. As wicked as what they done to Charlotte and the rest. That's what he said.'

'What *who* said?'

Tyler didn't answer. His brow furrowed, 'Guess I got some blame for what happened then, too. Hell, I sent men off plenty of times to scare the hide off nester folks. They never killed no-one, but came pretty close to it now and then. Men like Polanski and Cray was only helping their own. And they died for it. It was bad times, back then. A lot of hating.'

He swallowed hard. 'Hell, I can't blame Charlotte for running off from me. I was mean, I was angry. And I was goddamned wrong!'

'My Tyler....'

He ignored her. 'And it don't seem I learned much in all the years between. Willy Candell, Jude Wallis, maybe they did deserve to die for what they done. But there's a right way and a wrong, and I chose the wrong way.'

There was a sudden growing noise in that watching crowd, and unwillingly, Emmy turned to see what was causing the fuss. There was a rider coming slowly into town, and following behind were a couple of rough carts, pulled by mules, with a group of homesteaders walking alongside.

Emmy recognised the horseman at once. 'Buzz!' she cried out in almost painful relief. Tyler forgotten, she ran, pushing her way through the jostling crowd, and headed for him. He reined in his mount, and was out of the saddle by the time she threw herself at him.

He held her tight a moment, and then released her. Thickly, he said, 'It's been a bad day, Emmy. Your father....'

Her eyes were already going to the first of those approaching carts and she knew that those three shapes covered with sacking were the bodies of men, and that one of them was her father.

Then a single gunshot rang out, and she spun round, just in time to see Deal Tyler slump to the dusty street, with the weapon which had killed him, still gripped in his right hand.

She turned back to Broleen. 'I guess it's finished, Buzz,' she said in a low, hoarse voice.

Broleen knew there'd be another time to tell her about her father's dying confession, about the madness that had taken him and others over as Polanski's cabin burned. How they'd all agreed to say nothing, but how they'd all been haunted in one way or another ever since. It was all history now. The guilty men were dead, and the not-so-guilty. The town of Victory had been halfway to hell, but it was starting to crawl home again now. There'd be no range war in Brady County. So he said nothing, and put his arms round Emmy, and let her sob out her sorrow into his dusty shirt.

There were those who swore afterwards that there'd been someone watching from inside the sheriff's office; a big, shadowy shape, they said, just beyond that shattered window. But there were a lot more who recalled that they'd heard something just as the echo of the shot that killed

Deal Tyler withered away into the heat-shimmering air. It became part of the legend that old men told their grandchildren, how over beyond the distant mountains there was a low, throbbing rumble of thunder, and a far-away crackling flash in the sky.

And there was certainly no argument about the fact that the first, pebble sized drops of rain spattered down next morning on the mourners grouped round Deal Tyler's grave.

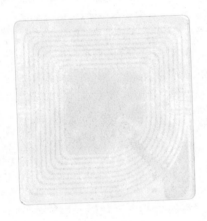